Dawn

Valerie Ford

Contents

Chapter 1 – Me

I was running through the forest with no idea where to go or where I am. Cold wind gushing and I was slashing through it ignoring the pain I felt. Everything was pitch black. I couldn't see a thing except for the glittering stars and radiant moonlight beaming on me reflecting my tattered clothes. I knew something was following me but I didn't stop even to check my bruised body and bleeding bare soles. I was cold and burning from inside due to pain. All I realized that I had to run... I barely had any power left but my inner conscience yelling at me constantly reminding me just to save myself and run...I could feel my heart beating very fast and a burning sensation in my chest eventually slowing me down. I stumbled on something and fell down and abruptly felt an ice-cold touch, someone, roughly grabbing my arm calling out my name...

"Serena"

"You'll be late again. Come on, get up already," a woman's voice echoed in my ears. I stirred from my slumber, relieved to discover that it had all been nothing more than a terrifying, unsettling nightmare.

"I'm on my way, Jasmine," I replied, shaking off the remnants of the nightmare and preparing to face the new day. I headed straight for the bathroom, eager to wash away the lingering unease from the nightmare. After a quick shower, I changed into my vibrant red uniform and readied myself for another day at work. Jasmine sat at the dining table, engrossed in her paperwork as always. She hadn't touched her breakfast, a sight that had become all too familiar in recent weeks. The stress had taken its toll on her and I could see the bags under her eyes.

She was the only one who I could call my family. When I was 6, her brother John, adopted me but he soon died in a car accident and since then I've been in Jasmine's care. I have no memories of him whatsoever nor did I ask about him much, it makes Jasmine angry. They must not be on good terms. Ultimately, I stopped bothering her.

I could smell the pleasant aroma of sweet honey and vanilla with a tint of strawberry all in the air.

"You are late. Hurry now. And while on your way give this box to Mrs.Stewart. Those are some cookies I baked yesterday. And ask her to pay today itself", she said sternly. I gave her a crestfallen look while munching the pancakes.

Jasmine had a side hustle baking cupcakes and cookies, which were a huge hit in our small town. But she had this unspoken rule of selling them only to a selected few, and I never really questioned her about it. She was always tight-lipped about her recipes and pretty much everything else in her life. Sometimes, I couldn't help but wonder if there was something more to those sweets, like maybe a dash of marijuana or weed, but I never dared to ask. Mrs. Stewart was one of Jasmine's exclusive customers, the only one I knew of. Her son, Jeremy, had been my classmate since junior high. He was quite the heartthrob and had a fan club of his own among the girls at school, but I made sure to keep my distance from him.

"I really don't want to" I protested, frowning. "Why do you always insist on going there? I don't like it."

"You don't have a choice. I have an important meeting with Mr. Stewart and won't have any time today. Also, his home is on your way to work", she sternly said. Aunt Jasmine was one of his assistant, well, I wouldn't call it an assistant. Her job was more like an advisor. He believes she possessed clairvoyance although it was more like a keen sense of intuition.

"Why don't you give it to Mr. Stewart then?", I argued but she shot me a stern look and then I reluctantly agreed.

I had nothing to say after all this, knowing she'll never understand. I didn't like Jeremy since he was in Junior High. There was always something unsettling about him, this creepy vibe that never seemed to fade. And after what he did to me at the Senior Prom, I just have absolute hatred towards him. Its because of him I feel uncomfortable towards men which is why I don't even want to date anyone. Right now, I just have to endure it and go to their house.

It was our senior prom. After the party was over and since it was late, Jeremy offered me to drop home. I agreed since I knew him but it was a grave mistake. In the mid of nowhere, he stopped the car leaving me frightened and with all kinds of thoughts. I was confused as to what happened. He drew me closer by grabbing my hand. His face looked uncertain yet determined. He then unexpectedly proposed me. I got startled by this sudden proposal. I somehow mustered courage and declined his advances explaining I never saw him more than a friend. But anger overtook him and he started forcing himself on me. I screamed and started to cry. I was helpless against his strong muscles. Seeing no way out, I bit him and ran away in the dark alleys. He followed me and managed to catch me while I tumbled due to my heels while he caught me again. I kept screaming but couldn't see a soul. Pinning me on the wall, he started to kiss me. I kicked him in the groin and ran away without looking back. Somehow I managed to escape and reached home. I wanted to tell everything to Jasmine but I was too scared to. What would she think? She thinks too highly of Jeremy's family. Also, she works as an assistant to Jeremy's father at his company. I didn't want her to lose her job. We aren't that well off so both of us have to work and if something would have happened to her job I couldn't think of how we would survive.

Jeremy knew of this as well so he always used to look for an opportunity so as to get near me.

I lived on the outskirts of Mariana which is quite whereas he stayed in the bustling city. I reached his house as big as a mansion gazing at the white sculptures of cupids. Every time I come here I feel like I've come to some palace. Big white walls with classy décor. I walked towards the gate and pressed the bell on the video answering machine. The gates opened automatically. I was just hoping not to see Jeremy. I could hear somebody walking through them from inside the other room.

A maid approached me ,"How can I help you miss?"

Before I could answer I saw Jeremy and his mother coming down-stairs. Jeremy as usual leering at me. I just wanted to leave asap from here.

"Hi, Mrs. Stewart. How are you ?"

"I'm great Serena. How are you doing sweetheart? You look so charming. I just had a talk with her. I'm glad to know you're prepar-ing for the entrance. Let me know if you need any kind of help", she flicked her hair showcasing her new set of rings. I wonder why do these rich people dress up in such a heavy makeup at home.

" Thanks, Mrs. Stewart. Jasmine had sent these for you. Glad you like them".I shyly stated and soon as she saw the box her eyes lit up. My suspicions grew stronger, I'm sure these are not ordinary sweets.

" I gotta go now. Getting late for work. Bye Mrs. Stewart". She waved me and Jeremy followed behind. I knew he was going to stop me. I just somehow slip away taking the worker's entrance.

It's already past 9 and I was dreadfully late for my shift at 'Steaming Mugs'. While job wasn't glamorous, it was a lifeline for our small town. It paid the bills and kept me occupied so I am grateful. I could see Maddy flirting with the new boy Rob when she winked at me saying, "Serena, you're late again. Boss hasn't come yet. Just start already".

" I'm sorry Maddy. I just had to take a detour today. Let's get to work" I said her without looking into her green eyes. She was a total barbie but a very good friend. The cafe buzzed with customers. My head felt a little heavy due to deprived sleep. I just want this day to end and crawl into the comfort of my bed. As I was serving, I heard a crashing sound. I turned to find out a customer, who accidentally slipped the milkshake from her hand. Seeing how awkward her face was, I swiftly rushed to her help.

"I'm so sorry for this mess," she said embarrassingly.

"It's ok miss. Please help yourselves with these tissues." I reassured her and proceeded to collect those glass pieces. One of them pricked my finger leaving me bleeding. I immediately regretted not using the stupid gloves. I rushed to the first aid and applied a band-aid. "Talk about a bad day," I whispered to myself and continued my work.

I came out of the locker room. I saw a tall, fair man in a black suit coming towards me. He paused as he came near and took a long breath before asking me "Excuse me......., Could you please tell me which way is the restroom."

"Straight from the next right," I said

He thanked me and took another long breath before leaving. For some reason, I felt his behavior a little weird. I ignored him after I looked at a long queue formed in front of me.

It was a bit tiring day. Since Ashley didn't come today, I had to cover her shift as well. I threw all the garbage in the bin, got changed to my jeans, tshirt with a jacket over it. As I started to walk, cold breeze gushed through me sending chills to my bone. It was very windy today.I felt as if someone was following me but I looked back only to find nobody was there. I just hurried walking at a rapid pace. I reached home in no time panting heavily.

Jasmine was as usual chanting some what I believe were prayers. She was never 'vocal' about her religion. I never saw a picture or idol of any deity, it seemed more spiritual to me. Not wanting to disturb her, I tiptoed into the kitchen and reheated the leftover chicken. I gulped it down fast as I was very hungry and then went straight upstairs, got a shower and changed into my pajamas. I heard a strange sound from the window. I cautiously went to check. It was a twig banging on my window due to the wind. I was too tired to do anything now. So I just went to bed and within no time I was in a deep sleep.

****

"Wake Up!" Jasmine said in a not so lovely voice dragging me out of the cover. And there she was standing in front of me with her long grey hair set loose. It was kind of scary.

I lazily pulled the cover back on top of me, " I wanted to sleep more. It's my day off."

I could see her face much more annoyed than before, "I have something important to tell you. Get changed fast and come down for breakfast. I'll be waiting" she said moving towards the door. It must be something important else she wouldn't even bother to come to my room. Sometimes I feel her harshness towards me is because I was burden. I turned the buzzing alarm off and woke up. I got fresh and went down stairs. My eyes laid on two big suitcases.

"What's those for? Are we going somewhere? " I asked surprised.

" I am going, you will stay. I wanted to tell you about it but last night you slept too early. Mr. Stewart is going on a business trip to Korea and since his secretary is on maternity leave I've been looking after her work. So I've to accompany him" she said hesitantly. Well this has never happened before. Since the day I knew her she has never left me alone for even one single day. May be she has realised that I am old enough to take care of myself, or maybe she is going on a vacation with her boyfriend and embarrassed to tell me about it. Sometimes I feel like she is having an affair with Mr. Stewart. Even in her forties, she look quite young and gorgeous.

" How long?", I asked.

" Three weeks. I'll be paid double for this work" she said convincingly.

" Ok aunt Jasmine", I hugged her and then left. She was busy packing. I was kind of upset. We were not that close, she was always very formal with me but she was the closest thing I had to a family. I've never stayed alone. So I was a little scared as well but I didn't want her to see it.

***

I went to a store to collect Mr.Stewart's suit since Jasmine had no time due to her packing. The store was pretty huge. Marble tiles with glamorous lamps and mirrors. There was a rack of suits everywhere. It was very brilliantly lit. A pleasant floral scent entered my nose as soon as I stepped in. The customers there look wealthy. Everyone in their formal attire. Suddenly a tall, dark boy came towards me "How can I help you, Madam?".

I stuttered "I'm here to collect Mr. Stewart's suit" showing him the receipt Jasmine gave me.

" Yes, just wait for a moment I'll be back ", the boy smiled at me and left for the VIP room. I kept my bag and scarf down and seated myself on the soft couch. I had a glimpse of the VIP room while the door unlocked. It was undoubtedly much more gorgeous than in the main hall. Suddenly, I noticed three men staring at me right from the time I arrived, probably wondering why this servant girl is waiting in VIP lounge.

"Here it is Miss", the boy handed me the suit.

" Thanks," I said and left. When I got out, I saw many luxurious fancy cars linedoutside. I plugged in my headphones and started walking towards home. I could sense someone observing me. This is what I've been feeling for a couple of days. I walked at a rapid pace without looking behind. It was already dark and cold. Someone held my hand and my sudden instinct was to cry out for help but as I turned to look, it was the boy from the store.

"I'm sorry miss but you left your scarf. I thought you might need it. I was calling you out but it seems you didn't hear due to your headphones. Here it is." he said panting. I thanked him and left in embarrassment. That was so awkward. I walked fast and reached home.

Jasmine had two more suitcases packed which were a bit strange. Is she planning to elope with Mr. Stewart was thing that came to my mind. I didn't question her much and just went to my room.

Chapter 2 – Matilda

"Call me once you reach Korea " I said while she was entering her cab wearing no makeup and her ancestral black coat which was more like a robe which she never let me touch it. It was one of the things dear to her. "Have a safe trip".

She gave me an uncanny look and said, "Watch your back" as he cab left. No farewells, no expressions of love, just the way she always was – a person of few words and little emotion.

After a long, exhausting day, all I really craved was a quiet snack and a chance to get some rest. It was a tough one, especially since I had to cover for Victoria today as well. So, I took the bus and got off at my usual stop. I was very nervous to stay alone. I have never been alone in my entire life. Jasmine was always there.

As soon as I reached home, I switched on the lights but they wouldn't get on. I couldn't see a thing. In a panic, I activated the flashlight on my phone, hoping to find the generator and fix the issue. Out of nowhere, I felt something brush my hand knocking my phone down but before I try to anticipate anything it vanished into thin air. My heart raced as I felt a presence in the room, but I couldn't tell if it was a burglar or, heaven forbid, a psycho killer. Without wasting any more time, I rushed towards the door in an attempt to escape which failed. The door got shut. I stood stunned in horror and amassed strength to ask, "Who's there?".

I heard footsteps slowly leaning towards me. I made a run for the window, tripped over something, and fell down hitting my head hard. Resisting the pain, I crawled towards the window but couldn't. The pain was agonizing. The footsteps approached much closer. I could see a dark silhouette moving to touch me. I screamed loudly, he covered my mouth. I couldn't find the strength to get his hands off me leaving me breathless. My head fell very heavy and so my eyes. Within no time everything got blackout, my body felt loose and I lost my consciousness.

****

"She must have had a concussion".

" I saw her. It was Matilda with her in the photographs. However, she wasn't there when I went. She must have fled."

"That crazy bitch. Now that we have this girl with us, she'll certainly come up."

"Did u call William?"

"He's on his way with witches."

"Chain her. We still don't know what powers this bitch she has."

I see, here's a continuation of your story with that in mind:As I stood there, my heart pounding in fear, I suddenly realized I wasn't alone. The voices I had heard were coming from the shadows, from people I couldn't see properly. I had been kidnapped, and the situation was growing more terrifying by the moment. I heard vague voices of men speaking. I opened my eyes slowly finding myself cuffed and tied to a big tree inside a forest. My white dress was tattered, body full of small cuts and scrapes. An intense pain was caused on the back of my head probably due to the fall at my home. Trembling with fear, I tried to cry out for help but my throat was dry. I couldn't muster any courage even to speak.

"She's awake. Did they come?" I heard a man yelling.

I saw three men along with two women near me. All the men had well-built physique. Two of the the boys appeared the same age as me with black eyes and pale skin. Both dressed casually in brown leather jackets. The two women were identical twins. Both had tanned skin, curly long black hairs and brown eyes. They even wore the same red robes. The only difference about them was by the side, they parted their hairs.

The last man was evidently the toughest of the three. Muscular, tall and huge, pale-skinned with silky black hair. As soon as my eyes met him, I could see his blood-red eyes. I've never seen eyes such as this. It felt like he's been possessed.

I was already shivering in fear and anxiety when I gazed at him.

"William stop!" One of the red women instructed him.

He abruptly shifted and before I realize what happened, I could feel his massive hands clutching my neck knocking me unconscious.

****

"William, cease your actions," Cassandra, one of the red-robed witches, commanded urgently. Her gaze shifted towards Jared and Levi, who promptly restrained him by gripping his arms firmly. He growled at them and tossing them towards the rocks like it was nothing. His eyes were tainted with bloodlust, and they knew they had to intervene before he unleashed his fury. Eva, the other twin witch, chanted a spell calming him down.

"I'll kill her. That bitch took everything from me. I'll drain her to death. I'll make sure to torment her slowly and kill her," he scowled on Eva angrily. Vengeance and Hatred had blinded him.

"We need to get back first. It might be dangerous here",I warned him.

"Where is Claude?", William asked controlling his temper.

"He's went for a feed", Jared replied.

"Is he for real. This is not a time for that. We need to leave at least by tomorrow morning max", I frowned.

"We are not going anywhere without Claude.Lets leave as soon as he comes.Till then we will wait", William said.

"Very well", I said annoyingly.

Its morning. I waited with Eva and Jared with the girl while the others went for a feed. These vampires sometimes just get in my head.Controlling my anger, I look towards the girl. She looked so fragile and weak awake and staring at us all with fear.I just hope everything gets sorted soon.

Soon I felt a presence coming from the bushes. I got alert only to find it was Claude.

"Is it her?", he asked while gazing the girl.

"Yes" , Jared replied.

****

(Serena's POV)

"Claude, Do you even have any idea for what reason we have come here? Or you just don't care because it doesn't concern your family,don't you?", one red lady snarled at him while he ignored her completely. He kept gazing at me.

"Cassandra!!!", William shouted at me.

I got scared seeing William who last night tried to strangle me to death.He was now shouting at this Cassandra lady for talking back to the Claude person.

Claude seemed physically massive and may be stronger than William. He had brown curly hair, slightly tanned pale skin with brown eyes.

"Never mind William, I am not angry on our little Cassie.What's the plan now?", Claude said.

"Lets leave right now.We would reach by night.", William said.

"I don't want to go anywhere with you people.Leave me.Please I beg of you", I begged him crying my heart out.

"I don't even want to hear a word from that disgusting mouth of yours". William roared at me and I started weeping even louder as I saw those blood-red eyes.

"Calm down Will, I've got her.Lets leave", Claude said as he wrapped me in his arms. Before I could resist, I found myself in sky in his arms.Cold air blew past us.Sunlight poking though my skin.I could see the lush green forest and river flowing beneath me. I got an aerial view of the whole outskirts. I found myself clinging him harder due to the scare I felt. I could hear him giggling seeing my state. My eyes went towards the two red twins, one of them Cassandra, who were flying on brooms like witches while the other men jumped extremely high from tree to tree. I knew these people were not normal.

"Leave me, please", I screamed and begged him.

He laughed at me and said, "If I do that,you'll fall to your death. We are feets above".

Saying this he left me mid-air.I saw myself falling down and let out a scream and eventually everything got black.

****

(Cassandra's POV)

We reached the Gregor palace by yesterday night and kept the girl in the west tower locked up in the room. I was too tired from the journey. I just had a good peaceful sleep knowing that we found our first lead to that bitch. I went to that girls' room along with Eva and William. The girl laid there trembling in fear looking at us.

"I'll just kill her.I cannot stand her presence" , William frowned.

"Let us examine her if she truly is Matilda's daughter or she has any protective barrier.Just give us some time. Unlike your kind, we don't harm innocent humans. I don't want to lose my powers because of this. Just stay put already. Let us do our work." Eva stated coldly.

He kept staring at both of us furiously but we ignored him and started chanting spells.

"zunipo coral sentizas subponatis"

"dazecsho parelu subponatis"

"Jon sta totozhnist' tsiyeyi istiyak."

I stared at Eva in disbelief. Everyone else stayed silent expecting our response.

"There's a shield that prevents us from recognizing her form. We could strongly sense Matilda's 'mana' all over her. There's no denying it. But that doesn't imply that she is what we think she is" Eva asserted in a confusion.

"We need help from the Reese family. This is some high-level enchantment we cannot crack just with the two of us." I started making it clear since we were helpless.

"Matilda's mana being there signifies the truth crystal-clear. I'll kill her myself", William snarled at me.

"I can't let you do that. Since this is completely new to us, it is a threat to our kind as well. We have to scrutinize this." Completely ignoring William I turned towards Eva, "Summon the Reese family along with their coven. Tell them about this crisis meanwhile, I'll search if I can get any clue on this."

Jared while gazing at the girl asked me "What to do with this girl?"

"I've already put a spell on her. She won't be awake for two more days. By the time we should figure out something" Eva flinched and left the room followed by William who stormed out while slamming the door.

I've never once seen William lose his usually calm demeanor in all these centuries. Hatred and blood-lust filled in those red eyes. I could clearly sense immense hostility in that powerful mana. Somewhere in my heart I still feel pity for him for all the agony he's suffered all these years.

"Jared, Levi keep an eye on her. I'll be in my library. Call me if you notice even the slightest movement", instructing them and leaving the room.

****

I was looking through the books with forbidden spells to find some-thing useful. Books after books but nothing that could help me. Suddenly I felt multiple manas coming from the southwest. It surely were the Reese'. Three manas felt prominent among them. I knew they couldn't say no after sensing themselves this strange girl.

"She is awake", Jared said entering the library.

"Good timing. They'll also be here in a couple of minutes. As soon as they come, take them to that room", I said still looking for the books.

"I'll go and call William," he said while stepping out.

"Don't bother. He might have already noticed their mana. Just go and get everyone to the room" I left the library to join the others.

I welcomed the guests, "Ada, Margaret, Ivan its good to have your acquaintance."

"Where is she?", Ada as usual straight to the point with her blank grey eyes whereas Margaret seemed furious.

We all went inside the room where the girl was kept. William was al-ready there biting his teeth. The girl was awake, feeble, and frightened laying half-dead motionless.

"I could smell Matilda from distant, and came here hoping to kill that wench. I'm not as happy to see this girl", Margaret scowled.

Keeping her composure Ada said, "Calm down Margaret, we all wish for the same. We should first check how does a person has another person's mana. And what exactly she is."

Ivan was quiet the whole moment carefully watching the girl as if he is trying to aniticipate something.

"I address all witches to gather around this girl. We would perform a 'hunaniaeth' spell on the girl lying here", I commanded the coven.

The vampires stayed far away in the corner. All the witches from Reese and along with Ada, Margaret, Eva, and myself encircled the girl and we started chanting unanimously.

"zunipo coral sentizas subponatis"

"dazecsho parelu subponatis"

"Jon sta totozhnist' tsiyeyi istiyak."

"zunipo coral sentizas subponatis"

"dazecsho parelu subponatis"

"Jon sta totozhnist' tsiyeyi istiyak."

"zunipo coral sentizas subponatis"

"dazecsho parelu subponatis"

"Jon sta totozhnist' tsiyeyi istiyak."

Suddenly, all the glass windows shattered into pieces. The dirt and dust caused a small tornado. Wind gushed heavily throughout the room. We still continued our chanting. The spell was too powerful to break. The cuffs on the girl's hands came off alerting the vampires into an attack stance. Luckily, Ivan prevented them from doing so. We still continued and suddenly some of the young witches started bleeding their noses. William was about to attack the girl who didn't move an inch and stayed there staring at the ceiling breathlessly. Ivan managed to stop him. Suddenly, all the witches including us four collapsed as chanting came to a halt.

"She's a human", Margaret screamed in pain.

" I don't think so. It must be a mistake", William mumbled.

All the young witches were knocked out unconscious. I, Eva, and Margaret felt immense pain in our heads. Ada was the only one who stood still.

"There's no mistake. She's a human, not a witch and certainly not Matilda's or John's daughter. Matilda's mana which we felt on her was just camouflaged. She's playing with us."

"Damn that bitch.." Margaret lost her conscious cursing Matilda.

"We have only deduced the truth about her form but Matilda's mana is still latching on to her. For what reason and how is this even possible is totally mysterious and I've no idea." Ada confessed.

"When I saw her in the cafe and getting information on her I got to know that she was an orphan adopted by John 13 years ago and as soon as he went missing Matilda raised her as her own. She stayed with her in disguise as Jasmine Rosewood ", Jared said as everyone stared at him in shock.

I got stunned hearing this, " Why would she bother doing that. 13 years staying with a mere human. And why would John even adopt one in the first place? Why would she go on placing her mana to her when she knew we would somehow know the truth behind it but still its there?".

Everyone panicked and as well as alarmed something about this girl was crucial to both of those evil siblings, the reason for which they kept her for these many years. Nobody had any idea.

"Let's think about this situation once everyone else is fine. There's also the matter with the Valacs. They aren't aware of all this crisis. Don't know how long we can hide this from them. For now, the wounded need help. Uncuff this human and tend to her wounds as well." Ada stated calmly.

"She's didn't have a single scratch, Ada. She's just weak", William growled in anger leaving the room.

Chapter 3 - Touch

(Serena's POV)

Everyone left the room. I didn't have any strength to move even though I was uncuffed. I tried moving my fingers but I couldn't. I felt too weak. It was just a miracle I was breathing. I didn't even remember how many days I've been sleeping.My body felt sore and weak. I laid there vulnerable and waited for death.

I recollected, I clearly heard them talking about uncle John and Jasmine who they called Matilda. Why were they calling her that? Does Jasmine know these people? Is John alive? What's their connection to these people?

All these questions were getting in my head. I had no idea what to believe. I could perfectly remember these people flying and jumping high with phenomenal speed.The women in purple robes and the Cassandra duo were definitely sorceresses, witches.

I heard the crackling of the door and a beautiful woman in a long white flooring dress entered. She was blonde, gorgeous, with pretty golden eyes, a pale complexion like the many others who weren't witches. She looked like a goddess.

"I'm Cecily. I've been told to help you change and feed you", she said furiously clearly stating she didn't want to do that. She carried me in her arms like I was nothing and moved at a superfast speed. How did she do that?

Within a moment I was in front of a door leading to a big bedroom with a huge bed. The bed was covered with purple satin sheets. The walls were mauve-colored with several paintings. The floor was a glossy white marble sparkling in the sunlight. She kept me on the bed and handed me a glass that had a dark blackish brownish thick-textured liquid.

"Drink it", she ordered.

I knew it was either poisoned or drugged. Refusing her I said, "I won't". Before I could run away from her, she caught my wrist tightly, pulled me towards her, and forced it down through my throat. It had a tint of citrus flavor along with the harsh bitterness.

Within a few seconds, I felt so much better, I could stand without her help. I wondered was it some magical witch potion. She handed me the clothes and shoved me towards the bathroom.

"Make it fast", she clenched her teeth.

I went to the bathroom. It was very huge and dazzling, bigger than the one at Stewart mansion. It had a massive circular bathtub and a shower area. Getting into the bathtub was a bad idea since the blonde beauty waited outside. So I used the shower instead.

I got dressed in the light pink frock which she handed me and got out in ten minutes.

"Stay in this room unless you don't value your life. Don't try anything funny", she left slamming the door.

I was very nervous and scared with no idea if I can even leave alive from here. I laid on the bed waiting.

The door opened and in came Ada and Cassandra along with Cecily and Claude.

There was one more man with them who was present before as well. He was as muscular as William and equally good looking with short blonde hair, soft blue eyes, smooth pale skin.

As soon as I saw William, I pushed myself towards the wall trembling in fear. Tears left my eyes as my eyes met his.

"We aren't going to kill you. We just need you to co-operate", Cassandra said.

"What's your name?" she asked.

"Serena Rosewood...", I said sobbing.

"What's your relation with Matilda?", she asked.

" I don't know who she is ", I replied calmly.

William punched the wall with full force with his huge arms causing a big hole in it. It caused a huge sound that made me jolt in fear and I began weeping even louder.

"Tell the truth or else I'll rip you into pieces", he howled at me.

I thought it's just over for me now. I'm gonna die. I didn't feel my legs as I collapsed on my knee and cried.

"She's speaking the truth. She doesn't know. I can read her mind. Either her thoughts have been wiped off or she really doesn't know. Or it is possible some sort of articular barrier or invisible enchantment marked on her body impeding us to know anything", the Ada said.

" I didn't see any ring, bracelet, or any other item when I took her to this room. All she had on were her clothes ", Cecily assured them.

"Ok. Then we should examine her body for engravings. Ivan, would you?", Ada asked the blue-eyed man.

As he proceeded towards me, my body started shaking in fear. I curled myself into a fetal position and started yelling with my hands on my ears. I saw Jeremy and I started screaming at top of my lungs and sobbing heavily curled with my knees to my chest.

" Stop Ivan ", Ada ordered.

"Ivan, Claude and William would you please go out for a moment", Ada added with hesitation.

"What the hell is happening? Had she lost her mind now? ", William frowned and left the room behind Ivan.

As soon as they both left, I got calm and left the witches to examine me.

********(Cassandra's POV)

We left the room letting Serena sleep. As soon as we reached downstairs, I saw Ivan sitting in a deep thought thinking something whereas William moving to and fro angrily.

"There aren't any enchantments on her body. It seems she really doesn't know anything. Now the only thing left is the mana...I would need to go back and research. It'll take a few weeks or months. I'm not even sure if I can get anything on this. By the time you need to keep a watch on her, " Ada instructed while leaving for east building.

"Its New Moon tonight. I'll be gone with the other witches in the East building. Ada has put a spell on Serena's room so that no vampire could enter tonight. I'll see you tomorrow. And Ivan is the only vampire here today from the Reese family. So that shouldn't be a problem", I said taking my leave.

******(Serena's POV)

I didn't realize when I dozed off. I could only recall Cecily dressing me up after the witches checked my body. I woke up in the same room. It was almost sunset. I went towards the window to look outside if I could escape. I could clearly see I would only fall to my death from this height.

My eyes fell on the huge green trees which covered area as long as I could see ending at a mountain range slightly capped with snow. I realized I was nowhere near home. A cold chill went down my spine getting me frozen. I rubbed my palms and closed the window.

A grilled cheese sandwich and fruit juice were kept on the table beside me. I felt very hungry and very thirsty. Without thinking any further, I gulped down the sandwich and the juice.

My gaze went to a big hole in the wall made by William. The debris was all over. It was abnormal. No human could do this even if he's a pro wrestler. These people were not normal. I just have to escape somehow. I would do it at night when everyone's asleep.

I missed Jasmine. She must be worried after being unable to reach me. I just don't understand why these people have mistaken her for Matilda. These people held some kind of grudge towards uncle John and Jasmine. I just hope Jasmine is safe.

I went to the balcony on the other side. I could view a big garden with numerous flowers and shrubs. I couldn't identify any flower. But they looked very unique. Forest covered this direction as well with huge mountains at distant. I was pretty sure we were in the middle of a big forest. Feeling empty and full of despair, I stood there stunned for hours thinking nothing. I lost the track of time. I checked the time on the table clock. It was almost 9.

I got distracted by the crackling sound of the door. It was a plum old lady in a maid outfit. She brought a tray along, kept it on the table, and took the previous tray, and left without saying a word.

A small serving of rice and chicken along with a bowl of bean soup laid there. I finished it calmly while thinking of how to escape. My initial plan was to jump through the window using clothes-sheet-made rope but it seemed so high I dropped the plan and thought of something else. Sneaking out through the door was the only choice I could see. I pretended to sleep as I knew someone might come to check on me.

I was correct. The old lady slightly opened the door and left seeing me asleep. Now it was just a matter of few hours till everyone else went to a deep slumber.

I laid there anxious looking at the ceiling. Every minute felt so long. I was heavily sweating due to the anxiety. What if I get caught? Even if I manage to escape this place, how will I get out of this forest myself?

I checked the time. It was past 2. I slowly got up from the bed and went towards the door. I tried to hear if I can hear anyone coming. But there was nobody. I held the latch and unlocked it slowly pulling it towards myself. The door didn't open. I applied more force but it didn't budge.

I was pretty sure there wasn't any extra latch from outside when Cecily carried me here. The door was probably jammed. I didn't want a silly reason as this to prevent me from escaping these monsters. I had to leave. I applied full force. It remained still. Mustering all my strength, I heaved the door towards me with both my hands. Finally, it opened giving me a ray of hope.

I checked both right and left of the big hallway. There wasn't anyone. I slowly walked towards my right searching for the stairs. I went down slowly. I could hear sounds of people moaning. As I went down, their voices became louder.

I walked down till the first floor and I saw people hugging each other. William, Ivan, Claude, Cecily, the two boys from yesterday along with a few other people. I couldn't see the twin sisters or Ada.

My eyes went to the floor covered with blood and I froze. All of them looked at me. They all had pale white skin and completely dark black eyes with their faces totally drenched in blood. The people they were hugging seemed lifeless with their necks bleeding.

William growled at me with his blood-covered mouth and I saw two sharp fangs leaving from his canines. Everyone else had the same fangs which left me hopeless and trembling in fear. A fear so strong I couldn't even scream. I knew what they were. I knew what they were capable of. I knew it was the end of me, they are going to kill me, ... those...

" Vampires...".

Chapter 4 – New Moon

Ivan's POV

Serena stood at the stairs traumatized by all this and collapsed in shock. Seeing her vulnerable, all vampires turned towards her to attack. She saw us with blank eyes full of despair and fear.

William growled loudly controlling his kindred ordering them not to attack meanwhile I went to her. She fainted on the stairs.

Her scent was too strong to resist. I somehow managed to suppress my thirst for her and gently grabbed her in my arms. Her soft velvety skin touched my cold hard body made me feel good. She looked incredibly gorgeous. Am I feeling my emotions too extreme because of the New Moon or is it because of her...

A loud growl distracted me, "I don't want anyone in the mansion until tomorrow morning. Disperse! ", William ordered and within a second the hall was deserted except for the humans that laid unconscious on the floor.

"Carry her to my room since we can't enter her room due to Ada's spell", William stood while looking at her.

I followed him to his room and gently placed her on his bed.

"How did she got out of the sealed room?", I asked him.

" I have no freaking idea. It shouldn't be possible. We cannot even call the witches tonight. Even the east building is sealed", he replied while his eyes staring Serena.

Covering her body with a bedsheet I turned towards him and said, "I'll wait with her till morning".

He snarled at me, "I'm waiting here as well. Even I don't trust you".

I couldn't trust this ill-tempered beast with her in his room. I just hope she is not involved with Matilda. Something was different about Serena. I felt at peace watching her. I could feel the presence of a very little almost negligible pure mana masked by that malicious mana. I was still unsure and I wanted to know.

William's POV

I don't understand why the hell is he waiting. It's not like I'm going to drink her dry. One thing was for sure both of us hated to stay seeing each other. He had never shown but he had as much hatred towards me as I had. I could feel it in his mana.

Its been only for this incident that I had to tolerate him for so long in these many centuries.

Our families are on good terms only because of the witches after what happened centuries before.

His eyes are totally glued on her. Does he feel something for this girl or he merely feels responsible? Well, I could only see him lusting over her. It's hard to guess.

She is sleeping peacefully without care after the stunt she pulled some time ago. If I wouldn't have been there, she would be dead meat.

She sure has the good luck to escape unscathed from a bunch of ferocious vampires that too on a New Moon. Ivan has also managed to restrain himself in all these centuries. He's in complete control now or so it seems.

Soon I felt something. I tried to focus and tried to sense what it was. I felt two different manas from this girl. It was tough to interpret. Apart from that bitch's, there's also another faint mana that was warm, bright, and pure. I had never ever felt a mana like this.

As much as it sounded impossible, I still felt.

Could Ivan have sensed the same...

Both of us stayed the whole night staring Serena. We lost track of time. It was morning and we could feel everyone coming.

Cassandra stormed in, "What the hell happened? How did she end up here".

Getting annoyed I said, " We have no clue. We were feeding and she unexpectedly appeared in front of us. It seems she was attempting to flee".

"That's not possible. I put a spell so that no vampire could enter her room for last night as well as a spell to prevent Matilda's mana to leave the room", Ada announced.

"Why didn't you put a spell directly on this girl not to let her leave?", I blurted out senselessly only to recall later that they couldn't.

"I'm sure you already know we witches cannot hurt innocent humans. Doing so would only make us lose our powers and I'm not so power-hungry to even resort to dark magic", Ada spatted angrily.

"Then how did she left the room", Cassandra said.

" I think Serena has her own mana", Ivan stated calmly driving everyone's attention towards him in curiosity and disbelief.

"But I can't feel anything", Ada stated closing her eyes in an attempt to sense.

"Me neither", Cassandra and Eva said in unison.

" I can feel..., I can also feel mana different than Matilda's", I murmured with everyone surprised, and Ivan completely astonished.

"What!!!", everyone yelled in surprise.

"We cannot lose her at any cost. Ivan, we need to leave and start scouring on this already", Ada said with a serious face.

"But just to make it clear, I'll be coming here every day to check on her. I don't trust the vampires here...", Ivan glaring at me stated this clearly.

" Suit yourself. I don't care as long as I don't have to talk to you.", I muttered.

"The feelings' mutual", Ivan replied.

" We would take our leave now. I'll communicate if there's anything through Ivan", saying this Ada left along with her witches and Ivan, leaving me Cassandra and Eva in the room.

"William, she would be scared to see you when she wakes up. I'll stay here with her and explain everything", Eva said.

" Ya that would be better", Cassandra replied.

I left the room angrily slamming the door. Why do I have to leave for that bitch's daughter or accomplice whatever?I would have killed her right away.

******

As I went downstairs, I saw Jared and Rose kissing right in front of the door. Both of them looked cheerful.

"Where's Claude?", I asked ignoring their special moment.

Jared unlocked his lips from her and moved aside from my way.

" I didn't saw him yesterday after you asked us to clear out. He didn't come with us for a feed", he answered.

"Some of the girls saw him going towards the north", Rose added while I left.

Why did he go towards the north? I don't think he lost control yesterday. I was distracted by Charles playing in the garden. Lifting him up I said, "What are you doing Charlie?"

He appeared sad, "I'm just watching these flowers. I'm bored. I wanted to play with Claude but he is not he", he pouted while leaving.

"You want big brother to play with you?", I asked.

" No..., I want Claude. He promised me he'll show me something interesting today but he just broke it", he said in a sad tone.

I knew that coming. Charles was always more relaxed with Claude even though I was his real brother. Maybe somewhere in his mind, he had my image as a tough, stern, overprotective brother. It was a fact but I loved him more than my own life. And Claude was more of like a younger brother to me even being elder than me.I'm glad both of them liked each other's company.

"And I always keep my promises, Charlie", I heard Claude jumping through the fence.

" Claude", Charles screamed with joy.

"Yes I'm going to show you something but first tell me did you feed?", he asked concerned.

He kept quiet knowing what's coming next.

"Martha?", I asked her.

"No my Lord. Little master didn't want to in the morning", she replied fearfully.

I lost my temper, " Martha how many times do I need to clarify this. Never let him out unless he's fed".

"I'm sorry Master. We'll go right away", she said with a low voice.

"Get out of my face. Take him and go", I frowned.

Both of them left and Charles agreed calmly to leave without any tantrums leaving me and Claude.

"Why did you go to the north last night", I asked concerned.

"Just some feeding...Too bored with these rusty people. I just craved some young fresh blood yesterday", he said while removing his bloodied shirt.

His appearance disgusted me but I was glad he was ok. Moving back towards the mansion I said, "Seems you had a big haul ".

He winked at me with a smirk, " You have no idea ".

We went to his room. It was very sloppy. Clothes stank everywhere, books, and shoes laid in the basket along with stained bedsheets. One corner of a room filled with stereos, speakers, and workstations with consoles hanging down through the table. The bed was covered with used towels, underwear, clothes, and blood. The room was a complete mess. There wasn't a space to sit.

"I'll need a shower. Make yourselves comfortable", he smirked and left.

" I'm taking the liberty to call someone for cleaning this disaster", I shouted while he was inside.

"As you please", he shouted back while humming some weird song.

'We'll bring you to hell

because we want to enslave

The soul will be frozen with fright'

Slowly the hums turn into loud horrendous screams. I could hear maids giggling and enjoying the show as I pulled out a chair and made a place for myself.

He stopped singing and asked, "How's the little lamb?", while he stepped out of the bathroom with only a towel around.

" Ladies you can leave... ", he winked at them while they left with a red blush.

"She's fine, enjoying the luxury of sleeping in my room", I replied annoyed.

" Whaaaaaaaaaaaaaatttt!!!!! You can't be serious", he exclaimed in utter skepticism completely exposed...

Chapter 5 - Past

va's POV

Everyone left while I stayed. Serena woke up abruptly due to the loud thud William caused.

As soon as she saw me, she panicked and moved towards the edge of the bed.

"Don't kill me, don't kill me", she pleaded and wept heavily. I felt pity for her seeing her trembling in terror.

"Calm down. We don't mean any harm. Just be calm and hear me out. Don't you want to know about your aunt Jasmine?", I said her convincingly.

I could sense curiosity as she steadied down.

"My name is Eva. I'm a witch. So is my twin sister Cassandra. We serve Gregors family for more than a thousand years", I paused as I noted her expression. Her face got pale with fright and disbelief.

" 1000 years? ", she questioned as if she heard wrong.

" Yes. Similarly Ada the one who was with Cassandra yesterday morning was a witch from the Reese family. All the witches you saw in purple robes were from her coven. Cassandra and I are the only ones from Gregors. William is our king whereas Ivan is the Reese king. Both Gregors and Reese are vampire families.

Everyone who you saw last night down are vampires.

Now the reason why you are being kept here is because of your aunt Jasmine.

Your aunt Jasmine who in reality is Matilda is a rogue witch that served the Bloodstones family of vampires.

The Bloodstone king Kairo was a very cruel, malicious, and power-hungry vampire.

He massacred William's parents, KingCornelius and Queen Arabella along with his little sister Claire.

He was not just happy with this much. He also killed Ivan's father and his three siblings including the future king, prince Isaac.

Both William and Ivan escaped their deaths because both of them were away from here.When they returned and saw what had happened, they went on a rampage in Bloodstone territory killing Kairo, his family, his kindred wiping them out from history completely.

The only ones left were their witches Matilda and John. They were given a choice either to join our covens or losing their powers. They silently agreed to join. John joined our coven and Matilda join Ada's".

"How old is Jasmine?", she asked skeptically.

"Younger than us by 200 years...", I replied calmly, "But little did we know about their real intentions, those backstabbing bastards fled with our moonstones."

"What is a moonstone?", she asked.

"Every vampire family has a moonstone which gives them abilities. There are four of them with Gregors, Reese, Bloodstones, and Valacs in four different shapes of the moon. So as of now, Matilda has three of them. Hence she has got so much power. Although, the stone is of no use to us witches since we already have more than the abilities that vampires get. But if she was still collecting those, she is up to something we don't know. She might have found a way to harness its powers for more than we could think of.

You are the first clue we had found about Matilda in the last six hundred years", I stated.

"Jasmine would never do that", she argued.

"She had done that. And you know what, she was the one who slaughtered William's sister Claire and Ivan's brother Isaac. But her being a witch was her only safe card. We didn't know the truth about their deaths until she fled else she would've had a tormenting death. I would have made sure of that."

"If she's your sinner why have you abducted me? I didn't do anything. I'm not even a witch or vampire. Also, I have no idea about moon-stones or anything", she said with her watery eyes.

"Matilda has masked you with her mana. This is something we have never seen ever in all these centuries", I said.

"What's mana?", she asked innocently.

"Mana is the sheer will power and spirit that the supernatural beings like the vampires, witches, werewolves, demons, have. Those with strong mana are extremely powerful. Even for mana not all supernatural creatures have.

On the other hand, humans don't have any mana except you as per William and Ivan. And they sense two manas not just one from you. One is that wench's and others are your own as they said. Parents have their mana masked on their children up to some years when they are very very young. But that's obviously not the case with you. Although how you have it we don't know since none of us except those two princes' sensed it", I explained.

"So what's going to happen to me now?", she asked frightened.

I calmly said, "Nothing. You just have to stay here and co-operate until we find any clue. Nobody would harm you not even the vampires as long as you obey."

She didn't reply to anything. She just looked at me in skepticism and stood frozen. I took my leave since it was better to leave her alone for some time...

******

Serenas POV

I couldn't believe whatever I heard. But the witches, vampires and all things that I saw since I arrived here, I just wanted to think of all this as a nightmare. It felt like I'm living a fantasy.

A knock at the door startled me. It was the fat lady from the other day who came with some clothes and a tray of food.

"I'm Martha. Here is your lunch miss. There are some clothes as well. Let me know if you need anything", she said politely while placing the tray on the table.

I hesitated but asked, "Are you a vampire?"

She smiled at me saying, "No, I'm a human like you" and left the room.

How could she be so relaxed knowing everything? Don't they attack her? My head was spinning with all this thinking.

I saw around. The hole in the wall was no longer there. I realized this was not the same room where I was previously kept.

This room was an exact replica of that room except it had a big white piano and a bookshelf. I grabbed my clothes and went for a bath. The bathroom was the exact size of the previous one. I quickly unzipped my dress and went into the bathtub. The water was very warm.

I laid there thinking about Jasmine. If she truly was the evil person Eva portrayed. Is John still alive? Too many questions were spinning in my head.

I got out and got dressed. She left in some inners and a blue long frilly dress. As I came out of the bathroom, I saw William searching for some books near the shelf. As soon as I saw him, my feet froze, my breath choked. He gave me a nasty look and left with a book, slamming the door.

I could understand the hatred he had for me but he was too frightening. Sensing he is not coming back, I went near the table. A small portion of grilled steak with some asparagus salad and a bowl of roasted vegetables were kept in the tray. I had it quietly.

"Can we come in?", a knock on the door unnerved me. Claude came in with a little boy who had black silky hair, pale skin, and grey eyes.

" Hi Serena, I didn't get the chance to introduce myself before. I'm Claude Valac and this is Prince Charles Gregor, William's younger brother".

Claude is a Valac...That was surprising.And the kid looked like a spitting image of his brother except for those innocent eyes...

"Hi, Charles", I greeted.

"She's so beautiful. Is she a fairy?", he innocently asked Claude.

" Yes...', Claude replied with a wide smile.

I gave a look at Claude. I still despised him for how he tossed me into air knocking me unconscious. He was also a beast but I didn't want to annoy him as he looked stronger than both William and Ivan.

Suddenly I felt a cold touch on my chest. It was Charles. He hugged me while burying his head into my chest. I flustered and got a little scared. Even though he looked like a 6-year-old, he was one of them.

"She's so soft and fluffy. Will you play with me?", he asked me with those puppy dog eyes.

" No Charlie. She's not feeling well today. Let's come some other day. Also, get your hands off her. That's not how you should behave with a girl ", he growled at the poor kid.

"So Serena, take rest for today... I'm sure you need it. If you need anything I'll always be delighted to help. Cya...", he said while leaving.

Even though he acted like a prick before, he was very warm and welcoming.

I picked a book from the shelf. It looked very fragile and old. I opened to read unfortunately I couldn't understand a thing. It was written in a foreign language. I checked in a few books. All were in foreign dialects.

Keeping those in their original places, I went to the huge balcony. It looked like I was on the first or second floor. I could see the main entrance with an enormous gate in the middle of a considerably heightened fencing. A big magnificent fountain stood in the middle of the vast lawn. Suddenly my eyes fell on a small monument. It was a sickle-shaped white marbled sculpture. Was it some kind of statue or sculpture...

I saw Cecily along with a few vampires, talking. They stopped chatting and looked at me. I got startled and ran away inside and bumped into someone huge. I gazed up to see William snarling at me in anger.

He clenched me tighter in his grip saying, "I can smell you all over my shelf. This is my room. You are not supposed to touch my shelf and my closet. If you do, I'll make sure you don't live another day. No matter who says what".

I couldn't say anything to him. I was very much scared of him. He was a vicious beast. Pushing me towards the bed he took off.

I buried my face into a pillow and kept weeping the whole night. Martha came with my dinner while seeing me pitifully. I didn't want to eat. I just wanted to leave. I thought of my previous life if I could ever go back and the thought made me cry more...

Chapter 6 - Cold

William's POV

"We're going for some fun. We'll be back by morning...W anna come?", Jared asked Levi and the others.

" Yes... Don't think I can enjoy the night here with these lyrical sobs. I'm already having a headache", Levi replied with all eyes directed towards my room.

"Cecily?", Rose invited her but she declined saying, "This is like a melody to my ears. I'll relish this moment". She had an evil smug look on her face while she left for her room. She had an extreme hatred towards Matilda since that bitch slew her mate on that dreadful night. She was patiently waiting for an opportunity just to have her revenge from the girl. So was I...

Everyone took off. The sobs were slowly turning into loud cries whacking my eardrums. The witches are lucky to not have sensitive ears like us I thought...

I heard chuckles coming from Claude's room. I quickly sped towards it. It was Charles playing video games with him.

"Why aren't you sleeping?", I asked him with a serious face.

" I just wanted to play with the fairy but Claude didn't allow me and he promised me that he'll play video games with me tonight as much as I want ", he pouted.

"Fairy?"

"The one you were hiding in your room but I saw her. She's so soft...", he replied.

I gave a glance at Claude as he ignored looking me in the eye.

"Charlie, it's late. Claude and I have to discuss something important. You should go back to sleep", I said sounding as much sweet as I could.

" Yes...Goodnight Claude", saying that he hopped happily out of the room.

"What did you tell him? And why did you take him to her?", I asked Claude controlling my anger.

"Chill she's just a fragile human and I'm pretty strong. Don't be so stiff... If she had any strength or powers, she would have already fled. And little Charlie thinks she's a nymph. We can't blame him, she's so freaking beautiful", he said carelessly tunneling his fingers through his hair.

"But still..."

He cut me and handed me the console and we played the whole night...

I could sense that mana. Why has he come now?

"It's him. Let's go", Claude said. We left the room and saw him sitting at the dining table with a glass of blood wine. Eva and Cassandra were having their breakfasts.

"I have a message from Ada. She thinks we should go meet Rowan. She believes he might have something", Ivan stated while looking at Cassandra.

" Ahhh, yes he might have something... But there is a high possibility he might not assist. We have tried so many times the last six centuries but he didn't help neither he accepted our apology...", Cassandra said with a face down.

"If only someone had control over their temper, we could get a clue ...", Ivan stated starting at me.

Waves of anger trailed through my body. But I calmed myself as I thought about it. He was a nasty vampire who lived along with his goons. He was a despicable pervert. I insulted him for leering at Claire. He deserved a good beating. But I went a little overboard blinding him in one eye in the process...

"What's done is done. Let's give it a try...", Claude mumbled.

"He saved Ada's life when she was a child and apparently she stayed with him for a few years hence she had asked him a favor", Ivan said while astonishing everyone.

"What??? Ada's friend??? That bastard???", I exclaimed in shock.

"How old is he?", Claude asked while a concern swept over his face.

Ivan while his gaze towards the floor said," He was 700 when Ada met him...So he must be close to 2000 years now".

Silence crept the room. He was much older than any of us. So he must be stronger as well. I didn't feel his strength the last time we fought. It may be because the moonstone was still there and I was much more powerful. But right now neither Ivan nor I had our abilities. If only Claude had any abilities, there was a chance we could overpower him.

"We still have to go. Claude, you also must come", Cassandra announced.

Determined to go, Claude said, "That goes without saying, Cassie".

"Eva you stay with Charles here", I ordered.

"Cassandra we need some sacrifices just in case...", Ivan said.

Cassandra looked towards me waiting for a response and I gazed Jared, "I'll take care of it", he responded.

"We'll leave after sunset. Meanwhile, I'll get the preparations done", Ivan said while taking his leave.

Jared gathered some human criminals as a sacrifice. Meanwhile, Cassandra dug herself into the library. I sent Eva to get the girl ready...

Serena's POV

I had my lunch and took a nap. I just wanted to escape from here. But everything I thought was hopeless. I saw no hope while being in this mansion under their surveillance.

Eva entered my room with a small bag.

"Serena get dressed. You have to leave", she said.

A ray of hope shined on my face but soon dispersed as she continued, "Sorry dear, I meant you need to go somewhere with Cassandra and the others".

My heart crunched in fear, "Are they finally going to kill me?".

Eva held my hands and convinced me, "No... They're just taking you to meet Ada's friend for some answers. Nothing else...".

Claude entered through the open door and said, "Babes, we need to leave in an hour. Please be ready by then" and he left in a hurry.

I got changed into the sleeveless black laced long dress while Eva waited near the bed. I could see something was bothering her.

"What happen Eva", I asked.

She hesitated and said, "Nothing".

I pushed her into saying, "Please tell me".

"You all are going to meet a very powerful vampire. And at this point, neither William nor Ivan has any abilities due to the missing moonstones. So I'm just worried about them", she spoke with concern and warmth. She was a very kind and gentle witch.

"What about Claude? He is a Valac. Isn't he? He must have abilities", I asked curiously.

Eva's face turned down as she said, "No he doesn't. Every Royal vampire gain abilities when they turn 21. But Claude was an exception. He didn't gain any and so was banished from their territory. Since then he's been living with Gregors and Reese. He's treated with the utmost respect by both the families. He's like a big brother or rather best friend to both William and Ivan."

"Big?... All of them look the same age...", I murmured.

Eva smiled at me and said, "William and Ivan are around 750 years old whereas Claude must be around 850".

I was stunned listening to this because all three of them looked like 23-24.

I went downstairs and saw everyone was standing outside ready to leave. I saw two black Audis waiting and a truck.

Claude and Jared hopped into the truck whereas William and Cassandra in one of the cars.

William faced Cecily, " Cecily, I need you to go with the girl", I clearly sensed the animosity from her. She hissed and went towards the other car taking the driver's seat. Ivan and I followed her. We took off.

I was very uncomfortable with him sitting so close. I shifted towards the door. I heard him clearing his throat.

"Hello Serena", he said in a deep voice.

"Hello, Ivan...", I replied in a low tone.

"I'm surprised you know my name". A wide smile ran through his face while I stayed shivering with cold. The heater was off. No wonder these vampires needed them anyway.

Sensing my body language he said, "Cecily, could you please turn on the heater". She switched it on while shooting sights of rage through the front mirror. It felt better and warm. I could feel her speeding up while still, her red eyes glued on me. I felt a surge in my heartbeats as I saw the indicator crossing 140 while still rising. Realizing I didn't put my seatbelts, I panicked while searching for those. Suddenly, the car flew off the road and landed with a big thud. Instinctively, I covered my face with my arms ready for the fall. But I felt a cold pair of hands wrapping me around my neck and waist. The car slowed down and I found myself clinging tightly to his massive chest. I quickly released myself from his clasp and straightened myself.

"Can you please drive a little slow?", Ivan said to her while she smirked with an evil look.

"Thanks", I expressed my gratitude while my eyes laid low.

I looked outside the window. Long trees covered on both sides of the road capped by snow. The bluish-purple sky was slowly enveloped by darkness.

"Ada? She isn't coming?", I asked him hesitantly.

"She is...She'll join us at the end of this forest... Are you scared?", he asked.

" A little... ", I responded.

"Don't be... I'm.....We're all there to protect you", he said convincingly as the car came to a halt at end of the forest.

I saw a hooded silhouette ahead of the truck next to William. Before I could, Ivan opened the door for me. A cold breeze swept through me making me quiver. They should've given me some coat or a jacket instead of this sleeveless dress.

I followed Ivan towards the others waiting.

"Leave the sacrifices here locked. We need to go deep inside. We can't get our cars in", Ada said looking towards everyone.

" Let's go", Ada said while she flew on her broom with others following her disappearing in an instant. I was left with Ivan alone.

He grabbed my waist and before I could say anything we were in midair.

"Hold on tight", he said as he jumped from tree to tree. I was terrified and cold. Closing my eyes I gripped him tightly while icy air gushed through us. I could feel my hair flowing in the air as we move and the hem of my dress raised till my upper thigh exposing me completely as we jumped down. So embarrassing...

After some time, we reached the spot. Ivan landed me gently, "Are you ok?".

I simply nodded and untangled my messed up hair. We stood on a plain ground surrounded by forest.

"Our little lamb seems frozen...Let me fire you up", Claude chuckled earning an intense gaze from Ivan.

He gathered some bricks and lit a flame. I quickly went and got some heat while the others stared at me. It felt so good. All numbness in my arms melted away.

Suddenly everyone glanced at the same direction with serious looks while Claude lifted me and pushed me behind him in a protective stance and whispered...

"He's here"...

Chapter 7 – Fire

I saw a few silhouettes appearing out of the woods. I saw a man in a white shirt who looked around the same age as Claude. He had long black hair, brown eyes, tanned skin, and a gym built physic with visible abs. The others with him had black hoodies covering their faces.

He stood forward from the rest and greeted Ada, "Adelaide... How are you dear. Long time no see... I thought..., no..., I'm sure I made myself clear I don't want to see any of those Gregors".

Ada pleaded him, "I know Rowan but we really need your help...", she paused looking at him carefully and continued, "Your eye... is normal... How? ...I'm delighted to know that you got your sight back".

Rowan while moving his fingers around his hair replied, "I've got some connections... I'm just glad to see you good and bright. However, I have no intention to help that bastard", he growled gazing angrily at William.

"Rowan, Please...I have waited for too long and we really need your help. Please...", Ada literally begged him.

" We have even bought some sacrifices...", Ivan interrupted Ada.

"Prince Ivan... My apologies...I just had my eyes on Adelaide I didn't notice your presence", Rowan said clearly mocking him."Adelaide now that the Prince has come here himself what can I say... Tell me how can I help you?".

"We wanted to know if it is possible for someone to masque someone else with their mana?", Ada asked.

Raising an eyebrow he said, "Why you wanna know that. As far as I remember that's dark magic".

Everyone glared at each other.

Ada asked him further, "Any idea how to undo that? Or anyone who can nullify it?".

"Adelaide in my entire life I haven't come across anyone with a masked mana...What are you up to?", he answered.

"Do you know any human who had a mana?", Ada inquired.

He started laughing loudly and so his group, "Adelaide you should stop hanging with these people. I think you had lost your touch and sense of knowledge. It's impossible for a human to have mana... Whose putting all those strange ideas in your mind", he said mocking her.

But Ada's face was normal as if she knew this coming. She said, "I want you to use your vision on a human".

Rowan stopped laughing with a stern look on his face. Claude pulled me next to him while still holding my hand. Suddenly a wind whooshed through my hand and in less than a second I was facing the others while Rowan stood behind me looping around my waist.

" Adelaide you totally know my type. She's too alluring and her scent is so addictive...hmmm", he said sniffing me while I was trembling in fear.

I saw Claude and the others gritting their teeth ready to attack.

"Please don't hurt her. She's not the sacrifice. They are kept towards the NorthEast. Please release her. We wanted you to use your vision on her to check if you can sense her second mana", Ada pleaded him.

Rowan held my shoulders and made me look in his eyes. I couldn't I was too frightened and my eyes were filled with tears. I was on the verge of collapsing while he held me firm.

" Mmm...I smell a virgin... Don't be scared love. I won't hurt you... ", he said with a wicked smile. I felt my legs numb as he pulled me closer.

" I can sense a mana on this human which reminds me of that beautiful Bloodstone witch... She was indeed a ravishing beauty...

Hmmm...what do we have here... There is another mana pure, innocent...Woah...Never saw this coming... How's that possible...

However, if you need to know how this girl got it you might get answers from the spirit of 'feu follet', but that won't be possible because I'm taking her", saying this he grasped me tightly caressing my neck while still sniffing me.

"No...Rowan, please... Don't kill her...", Ada cried out.

"Don't worry Adelaide sweetheart... I'm not going to kill this girl... Just keep her with me and have fun... Her scent is driving me crazy. I wonder how pleasant her blood will taste...", he said placing light kisses on my shoulder.

" Stop this, please...I beg you...Please don't do this... ", I wept heavily.

" Shhh... Don't cry, my love. I'll treat you very gently. You don't have to be scared of me", he said while pecking on my neck.

I got terrified and tried to escape from his grasp but I couldn't.

Within a second I saw myself on Rowan's left while Claude held him through his collar," Keep your filthy hands off her".His eyes were blood-red filled with rage.

Rowan remained unaffected and unruffled by his move. He pushed Claude with his right hand and the latter fall far off crushing a big boulder.

"You bastard...Don't touch her", Ivan said while holding a dagger at Rowans back. Before I could realize, I was too far from everyone near the edge of the forest while Ivan laid bleeding on the ground with the same dagger in his stomach.

I got totally horrified and let out a scream in shock...

" Leave her right now... ", William growled at him and threw a punch on him. Rowan caught his arm and twisted it like it was nothing throwing him over Claude.

"You have so many knights coming for you... It makes me want you more...", he said tightening his grip on me.

" Rowan...Please don't else I also have to fight against you", Ada warned him.

"I don't mind... You can't kill me, sweety. I can't leave this girl...", he winked at her shamelessly.

All three of them attacked him together but he just single-handedly dodged everyone smashing them down while still holding me in one hand.Everything was so crazy fast I couldn't grasp what's going... The next moment I was in the air while Rowan held me.

My eyes laid at Ivan who was healed completely ready to fight...As we came down, Rowan slowed down. It seemed like he was struggling to move fast...Seeing the opportunity, all three of them cornered us.

"Why am I slowing down?", he panicked.

" Because her dress is enchanted against you and I powdered it with some semialtus. Knowing you were such a perverted beast, I knew you would go for her. If you stay so close to her for any more time you'd be paralyzed", Cassandra replied.

" Rowan please leave her if you value your life. I cannot help you after this...", Ada requested him while Cassandra continued casting her spell.

He finally released my hand and whispered in my ear, "I'll come back for your kitty...".

Within a second he disappeared and so his goons...I kept trembling in fear near the fire. All of this was totally crazy. What if Cassandra didn't do all that on my dress. He would have taken me forcefully and...The thought of it ran shudders of disgust and fear through my body.

I couldn't take any more of this. I just had to escape from these monsters...

"Are you ok?", Claude asked.

I kept quiet.

"Serena??", Ivan called out.

I kept quiet.

"I can't sense their mana anymore... Let's leave", William said to Ada and Cassandra.

As soon as they turned towards him, I pulled a torch of flame and pointed towards them.

" Let me go...Please just let me go. I don't wanna be here. He'll come again for me. Please let me go I beg you all", I begged.

"What the hell do you think you are doing?", Cassandra shouted.

" Serena, calm down. We don't mean any harm to you. Please....", Ivan convincingly said.

"Serena...Keep that down. You'll hurt someone or worse yourself... Trust me please listen to me", Claude pleaded.

" He won't even touch you, Serena. I won't let him do that. Trust me...", Ada said looking at me pitifully.

Before I knew it, Cecily was behind me. She pulled the torch away from my hand which fell from my hand on her dress setting in ablaze.

She screamed in pain. I didn't do this purposely.it was a mistake. I tried to put it off with soil but it was a futile attempt. She continued shrieking in pain. Claude held me away from her.

"Illuminus pospenirus", Cassandra chanted

The fire went off and Jared ran towards Cecily.

"I knew you would show your true colors soon", William growled at me while raising his hand to slap me.

Claude stopped him, " No Will... Don't... She can't withstand... ".

" She was just scared...and what happened was just an accident", Ivan tried convincing him.

" I didn't mean to harm her... ", I whimpered.

" We should have treated her like a prisoner, not a guest", William howled at me grabbing my hair hurling me on the ground, and knocking me unconscious.

Chapter 8 – Warmth

Cassandra POV

I saw Serena rolling on the ground as William growled at her. She laid motionless in the dirt with scraped arms, soiled dress that got ripped from its hem till her thigh due to the smash. She looked like a broken doll.

"William... You bastard...", Ivan snapped at him.

Claude screamed, "Serena...Will...what did you do?".

Ivan ran towards her grabbing her in his arms while William left in fury.

"Is she hurt?", Claude asked Ivan.

"She's in extremely bad shape...", Ivan replied, " Cassandra, think you can fix her?"

"I don't have any herbs as of now and I'm extremely weak...We need to take her to the Gregor palace", I replied.

"Let's go...", Claude said.

Ada interrupted him saying, "Ivan, I'm sorry we can't join them... The Queen had called for you in the morning. Meet her and then you can leave for the Gregors...".

"Make up some excuse... I'll explain to her later", he said while his eyes still glued on Serena.

"I can't...Liam is visiting tomorrow", she said while both Ivan and Claude look astounded.

" What business does he have here now?", Claude exclaimed clenching his fists in anger. Ivan steadied himself.

"Claude, Please take care of her... I'll come tomorrow", Ivan said handing her to him.

"Claude, the Queen might soon call for you as well. As of now, you don't need to come. But be prepared...", Ada said before taking a leave. Ivan followed her after gazing at Serena for the last time.

Liam why would he be coming now all of a sudden. Did they know what we're hiding...It's going to be complicated. Or is it something else...

Ada and Ivan left. Claude carried Serena in his arms in one of the cars left by Ada and I went with Cecily and Jared in the other. I didn't see William when I reached the car. Cecily laid inert in Jared's arms waiting for me.

"Where's William?", I asked him.

"He left on his own...He said he would meet up tomorrow morning at the palace", Jared replied, "Her condition is growing critical by the minute...Will she be ok?".

"Yes, she'll be absolutely fine by tomorrow. We just need to get to the castle as soon as possible", I replied.

Vampires had extraordinary healing abilities but since this was an injury caused by fire, they couldn't heal. She was bellowing in pain.

Her legs were completely charred with small blisters. I couldn't do anything for her now I was already wearied from the previous fight.

****

As soon as we reached the palace, I quickly gathered the herbs and handed it to Eva.

"Eva, prepare a congelocion and apply on her legs immediately. I am very weak", I commanded her as I laid myself on the other couch.

"Hold her tight. Levi, you too...", she asked them both knowing the agonizing pain that would follow her every touch and Cecily won't be able to bear and could strike back in fury.

As soon as Eva started to apply, she let out a loud growl and shook violently screaming in pain. Her eyes were changed blood-red. Both Jared and Levi toughened their grip and pinned her back to the couch. As soon as she was done, Eva started the spell. She yelled louder raising herself from the couch.

In some time, she stopped screaming and laid stagnant.

"You can release her now. She would be fine by morning", Eva said in a low tone while Levi carried Cecily to her room".

"What happened back there and where is William ?", Eva asked astonished.

"Don't even ask. I need a rest. Let's go to my room", I was too exhausted to explain anything.

Serena POV

My eyes felt heavy. My bones felt shattered. I couldn't move a limb. I felt someone's arms wrapping me. I slowly opened my eyes to find myself with Claude. I tried to move but I felt an excruciating pain in my ribs.

"Don't move Serena. You're badly wounded. Stay still. We would reach in some time and Cassie would heal you. Just bear for some time...", he said cupping my face in his palm.

"It's cold...", I couldn't stop shivering as the cold gust puffed through my torn dress. He asked the man driving to switch the heater on. The man wasn't there when we came here. He had same glossy pale skin and a dull look. All I could conclude was he too was a vampire.

Claude removed his shirt and covered my legs. I still felt weak and cold and suddenly warm as I felt myself touching his exposed skin. Can vampires be warm... Ivan and William both had an ice-cold touch... But how was he so warm. I felt embarrassed when my face brushed his bare chest but the heat that I was feeling was like a flame flashing through my body. It was impossible to resist. So leaving my shame aside, I gripped him tightly to feel the overflowing warmth. Seeing my state, he squeezed me tighter.

"Serena, I'm sorry... It's all my fault. I didn't realize when Will grabbed you from my hands...Please forgive me", he apologized.

I could see sincerity filled with grief in those eyes... His eyes... They were black. Whenever I met him he always had brown...

"Your eyes... They're black", I murmured.

Closing his eyes, he took a long breath as if he was trying to control... When he opened his eyes, they were back to brown...

"Don't think too much. Just rest...", saying this he pulled me closer to his chest and I let myself into a deep slumber...

******

My sleep got disrupted as I felt someone poking me softly. It was Martha. It was morning already. I scanned the whole room but didn't see Claude.

"Drink this. You'll feel better", she handed me the same old bitter black potion. I drank it without any reluctance knowing it would work like a miracle. In some time, I felt better. My wounds were healed, the scrapes and bruises vanished. All that was left was weakness and dizziness.

"Prince Ivan wishes to have an audience with you...If you're unable to walk, I would relay the same", she said.

I wanted to check on Cecily. I wanted to know if she was ok so I agreed to go, "Ya I'll come right away". I had a quick shower and dressed up into an orange frock which she kept for me. I left downstairs and saw everyone at the dining table with Cecily who seemed fine to me. As soon as Ivan saw me he asked, "Are you feeling better?".

"Yes...", I replied

"I'm glad to know that", he responded eyeing my body to validate.

"What did Ada say about going to feu follet?", Cassandra asked turning to Ivan.

"Its a good spirit. We just need to get answers from it. Serena won't need to go. Let her rest... Only a few of us should go", he said while smiling at me.

"I'll go and Cassandra will be along...", William interrupted quickly.

"No. Since Ada is already there and Eva is better using spiritual magic she can go... I'll stay here. I need to check something in the library", Cassandra said.

"Very well....", William agreed.

Ivan turned towards Claude with concern on his face, "Claude you should stay here with Serena. I know that bloody Rowan...He wouldn't give up on her so easily he might come for her."

"Ya Claude, you stay here...we don't know if this girl would run away again...Let us cuff her. Cecily, you would be in charge of Serena while I'm away. Do whatever you want as long as you don't kill her...", William replied with an evil smirk on his face.

"I'll be pleased...", Cecily replied while gazing me hungrily. Waves of terror and panic rushed through my body as tears fell from my eyes. Claude quickly moved to my side and held my arms, "Will, she won't run away...I'll take care of that".

William growled in anger, "I've heard that many times and she had already lived up to my expectations... She's lucky she's not been thrown in the dungeon".

Ivan clenched his fists as hard that his veins were visible through those muscular biceps, "He wouldn't...Claude, tell him we're in this together...He can't decide everything himself".

William glanced at Claude and said, "My kindred had found her and right now she's in my territory. So nobody tells me what to do and what not with her...".

My eyes met Ivan's. His eyes were completely black and he turned towards Claude as though he wanted to say something. But suddenly, he got normal as if he was relieved. He came to me and wiped my tears and said, "Don't worry...You'll be ok with Claude here". I felt very relaxed hearing him.

"When are you going to leave and when you'll be back?", Claude asked.

"We would need to leave by sunset and won't be returning for a week", Ivan answered.

"A week????", Cassandra exclaimed.

"Yes... It'll take 3 days one way...", Ivan said.

"Can't we just take the jet", Eva asked.

"No... Liam was here... Luckily the Valacs still have no idea about all this... But I can't say for sure. So we should go by road...", Ivan replied.

"Why did he come?", Claude asked in a deep voice.

"A werewolf was caught in the west. He's been held captive by them. Liam just came to warn us...Fortunately, he won't be coming here. I said to him I'll pass the message", Ivan replied.

"We can't hide her for long. We need to do something soon", Cassandra expressed her worry.

"Why would he come alone though? They always travel in a pack...", Eva stated.

"Unless he was spying", William added.

Silence crept over the room with everyone gazing at me. I had no clue what they meant. I was just overwhelmed by the fact that werewolves exist. I just started wondering if ghosts, zombies, demons, and all other creatures do exist...

Chapter 9 – Flames

I sat on my bed, gazing at the mist-ridden foggy clouds, wondering if I could ever get out of this mess. I felt restless and anxious thinking of Rowan. Ivan said he might come for me. Just thinking about him sent shudders across my body. All three of them couldn't handle him together. How should I protect myself? From him? From William...I just want my previous life back. Even though it was not that great, but I was still satisfied with it. My job, my friends, my favorite bacon tomato double cheeseburger from Ted's. I miss it all. I felt an intense pain in my heart, and tears welled up out of my eyes.

A flipping sound startled me. I went to check the window but didn't see anyone. I heard a distinctive but melodious chirp towards the balcony. There was a faint movement behind the branches. It was a bird, a charming little bird with brilliant blue feathers, a long dark blue ribbon-tail. It flipped its wings and flew away. It looked so fascinating. It kept circling the sky for some time and then slowly descended towards me. I took a step back as it came close. It sat on the parapet glaring at me. It had incredibly attractive golden eyes. It slowly moved forward, walking through the edge. I could see his tiny feet with sharp-pointed claws. I quickly went inside and got some breadcrumbs from the leftovers of my breakfast and moved my palm towards him. He instantly flew off and sat on my palm. I felt his soft plumage tickling on my skin. He didn't eat the crumbs and instead started cheeping. I was intrigued as he started flapping his wings, causing a small wind. All the bits were cleared as he made a place for himself and sat down. He stopped chirping and looked me in the eye. I could feel his faint heartbeats on my palm...After some time, he abruptly stood up and gawked behind me and flew away...

I tried to see where he was but couldn't find him. My attention went towards the knock on the door.

"Wanna have some fun?" Claude asked as he entered my room.

"What fun?" I asked suspiciously.

"Video games...", he answered.

"I would rather take a nap", I replied him back.

"As you wish. Though I would've enjoyed a pretty lady's company, still, if you change your mind, I'll be in Charles' room ", saying this he winked at me and left.

I didn't want to go with him. Not that I disliked him, I was just not a video game person. He, on the other hand, was a lively person with a vibrant soul. He always looked out for me since I've arrived here... I felt very relaxed with him around. It was too early to call him my friend, but he was always cheerful and generous towards me, unlike that beast.

I despised William. It was more of a fear than anger I felt towards him. I understand his rage and a deep thirst for revenge, but I was innocent. But one thing I noticed there's one more person other than me whom he equally loathes. I never knew the reason, but I never saw them talking to each other directly. Even though they're facing each other, they spoke through Claude or someone else wholly ignoring each others' existence. Unlike William, Ivan was much of a gentleman. Though he seemed reserved, it felt like he was very mysterious. Apart from this, he was very kind and gentle towards me. Sometimes I thought him very overprotective towards me; however, I wasn't scared of him. It felt as if he like me by the way he used to behave, or maybe I'm overthinking...

*****

I didn't realize how long I slept. It was almost sunset. I felt a cold breeze blowing in through the balcony. I was bored, and there was nothing to do in this room, I thought maybe I'd take a quick peek at Charles' room. I went out of the door and strolled through the hallway leading to the left. I didn't know where his room was. I went on walking, hoping to ask someone. Suddenly, I felt two hands on the top of my shoulder.

"Boooohhh"

I got scared and let out a scream...

"Sshshhh...it's just me...I didn't know you'd be so scared", he said with a confused expression.

"Claude, You scared the hell out of me, " I replied, panting with my palm on my chest.

"Sorry, I knew you didn't know the way, so I just came to get you..." he replied.

I steadied myself. I was pissed at him. I was on the verge of having a panic attack. I could feel my heart beating in my mouth. In this short moment, so many scary things flashed before my eyes, Rowan's come to kidnap me, Cecily has come to know of me leaving my room, and the worst of all, William had came back...

Controlling my breath, I asked him, "How did you know I was coming"

He held my waist and, at full speed, rushed towards a room and whispered, "Your smell...You smell so good", he said, sniffing me. Creepy...

He opened the door to the mesmerizing view. The room was full of paintings and portraits depicting diversity in the era. Romanesque and Anglo-Saxon masterpieces styled on the right walls, whereas the center walls were decorated with Celtic and Germanic classics. It was mind-boggling. The figures in the portraits illustrated such strong emotions. I noticed the different arrangements they were kept based on scenes from heaven and hell. The ones from hell look very horrifying with demonic creatures devouring humans, blazing flames everywhere with bleeding burnt humans...

My attention diverted towards Charles, who came running towards me and squeezed me in his arms.

"Did you come to play with me?" he asked with those puppy eyes. I couldn't just ignore him. He was charming.

"Yes... These paintings are beautiful", I exclaimed, gazing them carefully.

"Our little Charlie is no less than Da Vinci," Claude said. I couldn't believe a little boy at his age could even accomplish this though he must be at least hundreds of years old. But I was still astonished by the work of those tiny fingers.

"Good, Charles... You're an exceptional painter...", I appreciated him tapping his head lightly. He pulled my arm abruptly, dragging me towards the console, sending an intense pain through my shoulder. Though he was a child, he had the strength of a vampire. Claude quickly grabbed his arm and stopped him.

"Charles!!!!" he screamed, "She's not a vampire. She is fragile. Don't hurt her," Claude gnarled at him. As he released his clutch, I could see the three red fingers stamped on my wrist.

"Sorry," he apologized with his gaze down. Lifting his chin, I said, "It's ok. Let's play... ".

We played for an hour. It was too complicated. I've never played video games in my entire life except for the one time with Jeremy in middle school. The games he had were full of violence, bloodbath, and all such stuff. It was similar to what I was playing right now. After an hour of continuous losing to Charles, I gave up. My fingers ache, and so were my wrists. Handing over to Claude, I got up and strolled towards the paintings.

A big painting caught my attention. A huge tree surrounded by a thick forest on one edge and a serene lake stood on the other. The brilliant colors of sunrays enthralled me. They were dispersed in enchanting hues of golden and pink. I carefully saw the figures sitting at the shore of the lake. It was William, Ivan, and Claude. All of them looked cheerful, even William, looking at a girl who was hiding behind the huge tree. The girl seemed incredibly gorgeous in her blue dress with her golden skin, long white hair flowing till her waist, and her red eyes clearly stating she was a vampire. She looked like a fierce avatar of a goddess.

"Who's she," I asked.

"Emma," Charles said with a sad expression.

"Ok. So Charles, why don't you sleep now. It's late. If Will comes to know he'll get mad...", Claude quickly changed the subject, and I realized I shouldn't have asked that.

" After some time...", Charles pleaded him, but that was ineffective, and Claude picked him up and laid him on the bed, ignoring his whining. I kissed him on his forehead and wished him "Goodnight Charles" before leaving.

Claude followed me back to my room, and I was shocked to see Cecily waiting for me fuming in anger.

"Where did you take off without my consent ?" she snapped furiously.

I panicked in fear.She was a beautiful yet vicious version of William. Before I could say anything, Claude snarled at her, "I took her... Forcefully... You've got any problem?" he smirked at her.

She growled at him back and left, slamming the door loudly. It was obvious she was scared of Claude. He was powerful and dominant.

We stood in the balcony gazing stars. I wanted to ask him about the girl, but I was too reluctant.

"Emma...You want to know about her right", he sensed my curiosity. That was so embarrassing, yet I wanted to know. I simply nodded.

"She was a gorgeous vampire, a fierce one, mighty...But she was a rogue. Those were times when there used to be a lot of rogues all around the continent. They had no control over their thirst and were on a killing spree. Ivan, William, and myself were sent to eradicate them. Rogue was also one of those... She was extremely powerful. Though she was not a royal, she still had powers. She could teleport, the only one known who could teleport...

We kept following her for almost a year and were finally able to ambush her. But we couldn't kill her... Both Ivan and William had started to like her... She played hard to get, which both of them found challenging. They didn't kill her on the promise that she doesn't go on killing humans."

"So you vampires don't kill humans, "I asked.

"We do...Only if they're bad or learned our secret...Else we form contracts with them in return for blood", he replied

That was surprising. I didn't expect this. I thought all of them were blood-thirsty vicious beasts...

"So what happened to her. Where is she now?"

Claude sighed gazing the floor,"Everything was good. We would sneak from our castles and meet her far away from here. Even though she had a fierce aura, she was extremely friendly and had managed a reasonable control of her thirst in a few months. I liked her as a good friend, but Will and Ivan developed feelings for her. The three of them were like inseparable.

One night a big fight ensued between them for who'll claim her. Both of them were like childhood best friends, like even before I came to stay. Seeing them fight, she tried to make them stop, but it was futile.

Earth felt tremors due to their wrath. Their strong manas clashed with such intensities that everything surrounding them was on fire. She still made an effort to make them stop, but they were blinded by rage.

Ultimately, she threw herself into those flames. She couldn't bear watching them kill each other for her. All we could hear were her painful screams, and all that remained back were ashes in the earth...It was the same dreadful night when Kairo massacred everyone here...."

Chapter 10 – The Board

I was totally stunned by what i just heard. Why did she kill herself? That too on same day... It must be so painful for them.

Claude continued, " Since that day, Ivan and William hadn't talked to each other. Ivan, who was so fun-loving and garrulous, became a reserved man, and on the other hand, William was consumed by anger. I never saw him smile since that day..."

I could see him in pain and grief. "It's so sad. I'm so sorry for I reminded you all that...", I apologized.

" It's ok. I'm fine... My pain is nothing compared to what both of them are enduring", Claude replied with a controlled expression.

Who would've imagined they had such a tragic past. Seeing the one you love, dying in front of your eyes, must be heart-wrenching. They lost all their loved ones on the same day. I cannot even imagine the agony they must be feeling. That explains the sorrowful expression I felt from Charles when I asked about Emma.

"Charles knew?", I asked.

"Yes... She use to like him a lot. He reminded her of her dead younger brother...", he replied.

Suddenly it clicked me and I let it out, "This was around six hundred years ago. So how come Charles is still a child?".

Claude steadied himself and looked towards me with a light smile,"The way we vampires age is very different. We grow like humans till we come of age, and then we age very slow around a year once in 50-70 years or 100.

And also moonstones do play an essential role in how we grow. The day moonstone was gone, Charles also stopped aging physically as well as psychologically."

"Ohh... That's very intense...", I replied. My feeble mind was unable to process so much information at once...

I felt Claude's warm hand cupping my face gently as he said,"Don't think too much...It's late. You should sleep now...". He covered my body with the comfy sheets and closed all the windows and took his leave before glancing at me one last time....

*****

It was almost two days. Everyone was gone. I spent it with Claude and Charles playing video games although I didn't like it much. But I was very bored.

The only thing I enjoyed was Claude's cooking. Cheese bacon risotto, mushroom ravioli, butter chicken were incredibly delicious. But the best one was a beef casserole. And it was all for me since the vampires mostly had blood and rarely had human food. Claude had outstanding culinary skills. The food he made was too flavorful.

I quietly savored an egg Benedict which he made today. The rich, creamy sauce perfectly complimented the butter streamed eggs. Both Charles and Claude gazed at me. Their faces seemed amused at this.

Claude suddenly stopped smiling and gazed towards the main door while I had my breakfast. It was the same man who escorted us that night after Rowan's scene. I wasn't able to see his face that night. He had glossy pale skin and brown hair, a perfect jawline, and a good built similar to Claude. As he came close, I saw a dull look in his grey eyes.

"Good morning Lord Claude," he greeted Claude while staring me.

Claude appeared annoyed and said, "Do not call me that... Martin, How many times do I need to tell you that".

Martin replied, "I'm afraid I cannot follow that, my Lord. Princess Irene wouldn't be happy." I felt his unpleasant stare directed towards me.

I could see a shift in Claude's expression as he heard Martin and continued, "So what brings you here."

"Our Queen wishes to see you," he replied, bowing his head at Claude.

"What a timing...", Claude expressed his disappointment. He didn't want to go it seemed.

Claude turned towards me and said, "I'll have to go. I can't avoid this, Serena...".

"Which Queen is he talking about," I asked curiously grabbing Martins attention.

"Queen Evelyn...Ivans mother...", he replied.

"But I thought Kairo killed her", I read my mind and bit my tongue at my stupidity...i felt a low growl from Martin who was clearly pissed.

Claude quickly answered, "No, no, no... Luckily, the queen and Princess Irene were at the Valacs Palace on that dreadful day... ".

I could still feel those dull grey eyes locked on me, annoyed but for what. It was not because of the comment I just made. I felt his unpleasant aura right from the moment he entered.

I didn't want Claude to leave."When you'll be back?" I asked.

"By tomorrow... Don't worry. Nothing would happen...", he assured me while his hands held mine. I didn't want him to go. He was my only friend here. My body felt nervous, thinking about Cecily, and I started trembling in fear. I was terrified at the thought of me having to stay alone here with 'she-William.'

Claude pulled me in his arms and gave me a tight hug. I could feel the warmth from his body, relaxing me...Martin gazed at us in astonishment as well seemed annoyed.

Claude left with Martin as I stood there watching till I couldn't see him anymore.

*****

Cecily came downstairs with an evil smirk. The moment I saw her, I realized I'm donefor. My heartbeat increased with every step she came down. Claude was the reason I was safe from her wrath until now. But now that he's gone, there's nobody to save me from her clutches.

"My friends are coming tomorrow. I want the hall and stairs clean and shining. All the humans are on leave, so you have to handle it yourself, and if you take anybody's help in this, you will regret it, and I will make sure of that..." she ordered me. I stood there, stunned by what I was hearing. I didn't know what I should reply. She hauled me towards the janitor room and tossed me on the floor. I felt extreme pain in my elbows and knees as I clashed on the marble tiles.

"If I see even a speck of dirt, you are dead meat." Saying this, she left slamming the door on my face.

I curled myself on my knees, trying to understand what just happened. There is no way all the helpers could be on leave on the same day. She is just trying to torture me, but I cannot protest. I just have to endure somehow until Claude comes; otherwise, she will torment me much more.

I grabbed the mop and began cleaning. The hall felt never-ending. It took me two hours to mop just half of it. I felt a sharp pain in my back and shoulders, and my back and hairs were drenched in sweat. I could feel the blood gathered beneath the flesh of my palm.

My gaze went through the sparkling polished marble floor. It shined as the sun rays reflected through its surface. All at the cost of my sweat and blood...

Every step felt heavy as if I'm dragging myself away from strong gravitational pull. My body reeked of citrusy phenyl. I entered the bathtub and was relived as the hot water robbed me of my pain and senses...

******A brilliant flash of light smashed on my face. I woke up to see the sun at its max. My body felt broken as I tried to lift myself from the bed.

My eyes never left the main door as I kept waiting for him. I missed him like a child waiting for his mama. A shrill sound of a speeding black car caught my attention. It was followed by a midnight blue one and a jeep with some men. My heart raced in desperation and anxiety at the thought of Claude being in one of them. I saw a few women coming out of the car ramping like supermodels. There were a few men as well, but my eyes surveyed only for Claude. I felt utterly disappointed when I saw the vehicles moving towards the parking lot. Those were the guests.

My stomach craved food. I didn't have anything since last night, and I was too hungry. I grabbed an apple from my table and surged towards the kitchen. To my surprise, it was empty. All the shelves and cabinets deprived of food. I ran towards the smaller refrigerator. It was as good as new with nothing inside.

I knew the other bigger fridge was filled with blood pouches. A sense of disgust and fear overtook me. I didn't even dare to cross-check.

Where did all the food go? Was it moved somewhere for the guests? It felt like the kitchen was ransacked. The apple was not enough to subdue my starvation. A crackling sound diverged me away from my thoughts. As I turned back, I felt a burning slash of pain on my cheek as my face rolled unknowing what had happened. Why did she smack me?

"You bitch... Can't you do one thing properly? I told you not to leave even a speck of dirt and yet...", Cecily growled at me angrily.

" But I did....", I tried to speak, but another slap followed, knocking me down.

"Just shut your crap...The guests are down. Get the blood wine from the fridge and serve them. And don't mess up", she left unleashing her fury. I did clean it properly. How did it get dirty? Knowing she wouldn't even listen to my explanation, I didn't bother to speak anything. Her slaps felt like two big bells violently striking in my skull. My left cheek was visibly red compared to my right one.

I didn't want to piss her off more than she already was. I took the goblets and lined them up. Opening the door, I pulled a handful of pouches of that thick bloody beverage and emptied it down the glasses. My stomach churned at that sight. Somehow I managed to carry the tray and went towards the hall.

"Is it her?" one of the girls asked Rose, who stood close to Jared. Rose nodded while staring at my direction. I noticed it wasn't just her but every one of them staring me. All the girls very beautiful; all of them have the same characteristic pale skin. The girl who asked about me had short red curls, which complemented well with her red eyes and red gown. What's with all the red...

"Just ignore that pest, Scarlett, and continue what you were saying," another girl in short blue dress said, scornfully looking at me.

Scarlett... That explains all the red...

"He was too handsome. His long silver hair streamed through his shoulders. I couldn't take my eyes off his cerulean blue ones. His smooth velvety skin twinkled like diamonds under the moonlight bestowing his magnificence... His beauty was breathtaking..." she said slowly, panting while the other girls watched her in awe. Human or vampire girls, I could find a similarity between them when it comes to men.

"What else you expect from a prince...", Cecily replied, however, her face was stone cold derived of any pinkish charm the other faces had. It was evident that she was not interested in the 'prince.' "When did he come back?" she added.

" Last week... That too, after so many centuries. Nobody has seen him except his family...Even Prince William has never seen him..." Scarlett said with a sparkling gaze in her eyes as I left towards the kitchen to fill the tray.

I walked towards the group of men standing in a circle laughing. I felt a bit awkward and uncomfortable with every step I took towards them.

"There's going to be a power surge among the Valacs, now that their rightful prince had returned...", a man with dark pale skin said.

Here again... the prince talk... Sounds like he's someone significant ...Claude might know since he's too a Valac.

I reached and started serving them with my gaze downwards. I didn't want any unwanted attention from these beasts. It was better just to ignore them.

"Who is this new butterfly?" a reddish haired man glared me. The similar red clothes and red eyes resembling Scarlett.

"She's the board...".

Chapter 11 - Bullseye

Serena's POV

I stood there listening to Cecily while others circled me. All of them had evil smirks on their faces. Are they going to kill me finally? Am I going to die now? My heart pounded fast in my chest. My breath suddenly felt deprived of air.

William had commanded her not to kill me. So why...

Waves of panic and fear swept across me as I speculated what was happening. They surrounded me like a pack of wild animals that corners its prey. The females added the bunch, and all the eyes were focused on the center at me.

I started to cower, and tears welled up in my eyes. My eyes latched up at the main door hoping that Claude would show up any second now. But he wasn't there.

I cried out for help, but all my cries fell on deaf ears. I expected at least Cassandra would show up, but she didn't.

Blood dripped down from the glasses on the tray as my hands shook violently in fear. As Cecily strode towards me, I wavered two steps behind until my back landed on a cold hard surface. I turned to see the red-haired man behind me with his hands on my waist. I instantly shuddered them away and kept a distance while he kept leering me.

"Don't you think she's too adorable for being the board?" he said.

"Come on, Scott. She's just putting an act. She's wicked to her core..." Cecily grimaced in anger and pulled the tray out of my hand, and placed it on the nearby table.

"Yes, brother. She set Cecily aflame a few days ago", Scarlett spatted as all the red eyes widened and gave me a scornful look. I didn't do it purposely. It was an accident. I wanted to yell out and prove my innocence but I realized it would be futile. So I just kept mum and instead beg for mercy.

Holding my wrist tightly, she dragged me out. I tried to shook away but she was unquestionably powerful. I was taken to the smaller garden next to the left corridor and tied to a tree. A small table stood next to me with two cases, silver, and black. All of them followed Cecily and stood at a distance while she walked towards me and diverged at the table.

I was shocked to see the pointed nail-like things inside. The silver case had long silver darts with sharp tips and considerably long shafts. My eyes were stuck to the silver case as horror crept over me, and I realized what it meant when she referred to me as a 'board' - ' a dartboard.'

"No... Please, No... I'm sorry... Please don't do this", I begged comprehending what was about to take place. She closed the case, and suddenly I felt relief. Did she take pity on me? Did she forgive me? Did she do all this just to scare me?

My relief was temporary, and fear overtook my senses as I saw her hand shifting towards the black case. It had blackish metallic darts with short shafts and small thin tips.

"Consider yourself lucky you're not a vampire or a wolf that we have to use these tiny babies," she said and turned towards the others while taking the case with her.

"So here are the rules," she continued while I stood there in despair. I gazed towards the gate and east building but still no sign of Claude or Cassandra. I tried undoing the ropes, but the knot was too tight. Even if I try to make a run for it, they'll capture me instantly with their supersonic speed.

"Ok, the usual rules are not applicable today. We're keeping it simple. Unfortunately, my orders do not allow me to kill her.

Everyone gets a single dart. The target area is her legs, and the knees are bullseye. I want her to feel the same pain I suffered when she burnt my legs—the one who manages to hit her from this distance with maximum fatality wins", she explained to them the 'rules' which left me stunned.

"Good. But I still think it's more fun with the wolves", Scarlett said.

The blue dressed girl who called me a pest earlier opposed, "I don't agree with you, Scarlett. Even if we can't kill her, it'll help us enhance our focus".

"Ria...Optimistic as always," a pale boy in a brown shirt sighed.

"Cecily, I think you're going too far. She's a human," Rose said protesting against this show.

"Well, I don't think so. If you can't handle this you can very well leave" she replied, utterly ignoring her. I saw Jared and Rose leaving before giving me a pitiful look. And there went my last support.

"So, who'll go first?" Cecily asked, and some of them volunteered, eventually Scarlett being chosen. She handed a dart to Scarlett, and everyone turned towards me. Some of them were cheering on her like this was some sort of game. I stayed still mentally preparing myself. Beads of sweat exuded from my forehead and rolled down, tracing my neck. Inhaling a deep breath of air, I held it, somehow in the back of my mind I felt, it might reduce the pain. She took a stance with her sight, targeted at my feet, dart parallel to her ear, and threw it while I immediately shut my eyes.

After a few seconds, I slowly opened my eyes. She screamed, "Shit...I missed,". I scanned my eyes nearby, but I didn't see the dart. Luckily I was unharmed. I prepared myself for the next one. It was a man in a white t-shirt. He aimed, and I closed my eyes again. I screamed as I felt a sharp pain in my left thigh. I gazed down to look at my bleeding leg. It hurt so much I couldn't bear another one. I started begging for mercy, but my voice couldn't be heard where they were rejoicing themselves.

I let out a loud wail in pain as the darts keep coming and piercing through my skin, not just my lower body, but some of the 'missed shots' grazed my arms as well. One of the darts stuck deep inside my right arm caused excruciating pain. The darts keep coming, and I continued crying in agony.

"I'll pass. I cannot hurt a girl as gorgeous as her", Scott said while his eyes gazing me.

"Great... I'll have your turn. I'll make sure to hit this time", Scarlett replied with her sparkling eyes.

Scott carelessly threw the dart, which fell near his feet and winked at Scarlett," Oops... I missed".

"Brother...", Scarlett screeched in anger while Scott smirked at her.

Next was Ria's turn. She focused and threw her dart, which penetrated and stuck on my right knee, making it difficult for me to stand. It was the most painful and unendurable injury so far.

"Bullseye!!!!"

I heard them all screaming and applauding, giggling and praising her while I stood there with my clothes tattered and soaked in blood, two of darts still stabbed in my flesh.

"Ok, so now that you are done, I'll deliver the final blow. I hope to get a bullseye", the host of the party said while gazing towards me right in my eye.

A shooting pain felt in my belly as I saw down, I was fully draped in blood, and my vision was getting blurred. Black spots cloaked my sight. My eyes felt heavy and my head felt drowsy.

" Ouch...I missed," were the last words I heard before darkness over-took me.

****

My eyes slowly opened as sun beamed radiantly on my face. It was not too long for I was unconscious. I was still tied to the tree with the darts inside me. Scarlett, Levi, and Rose stood in front of me with their backs turned. It seemed they were growling at something. I was unable to get a peek at what it was. It felt like they took a protective stance, but why towards me when they were the ones who hurt me.

I saw Levi, who was at the center, pushing a huge boy towards the grass. I got a glimpse at the brawl that took place ahead of him: Jared, Cecily, Scott, and Ria were fighting a few vampires.

Just what happened in this short period. Why are they fighting amongst themselves? A few minutes ago, they were cheering on each other to hurt me...

"Calm down and control," Scott said to a male vampire who seemed very muscular and had dark, frightening black eyes. When I looked at the others, all of them had same black eyes and a mysterious aura except the ones who were trying to protect me.

"We're just trying to help you. We don't want to hurt you ", Cecily added.

A girl and boy tried to attack me out of nowhere but Scarlett and Levi managed to hold them and threw them away.

" This human has a masked man on her. If you try to drink her blood, let alone taste it, I can't control what would happen next", Cecily announced, gazing them while the others calm down. They were breathing heavily, and their dark gazes were fixed on me.

Levi stood firmly ahead of me and said in an authoritative tone, "If you value your lives, you'll leave right at this moment. I'll not repeat myself."

Cecily glared at Levi in anger, but he completely ignored her."Leave now...", he said again. The crazy vampires start falling back and within a few seconds cleared, leaving me with the others.

Everyone stood in their places, gazing at different directions for a few minutes.

"They're gone," Scarlett said.

"Cecily, you said you had invited only those who had a reasonable control on their mana, didn't you?", Levi fumed in anger.

" Yes. They are all in complete control of their mana. I'm confident, and that's the reason I only invited them. I don't know how and what happened to them, "Cecily seemed confused.

"Don't give me all this crap. I know William assigned you in charge, and I even warned you before throwing a party," Levi stated.

" I know. These vampires are my friends for more than four centuries. I've known them. Like me, they also never drink from humans direc tly...not even by forming contracts like how it's done here in Gregors family. They only get it from pouches or animals. I don't understand what happened today", Cecily confusingly said, but as soon as my eyes met hers, I could see the unrest replaced by rage.

"We were outnumbered. They could have easily killed her, the only link to Matilda. And then what you would have done", Levi spatted.

"I think it's not Cecily's fault nor the uncontrolled vamps fault. It's the butterfly...Her blood...Her blood even drove me crazy, as I've never felt before—a thirst for a craving that's almost unimaginable to curb. I only know how I managed to stay calm and focused," Scott said, gaping me.

"Me too...I felt the same. You, Ria?" Scarlett added, and Ria nodded in reply.

"I also felt the same, but I thought it's because I didn't feed enough," Cecily added.

"Us too," Rose also stated.

Chapter 12 - Company

Serena's POV

Levi turned towards me. He pulled out the knots which held me standing. As soon as he untied me, I collapsed, but he grabbed me. He whispered slowly in my ears, "This might hurt a little" and removed the two darts. It was extremely painful.

Blood oozed out from them. I couldn't walk because my legs were in terrible shape. He lifted me and left.

Levi carried me here back to William's room and gently placed me on the bed and left and returned with a small first aid kit.

"There aren't any humans today, so you have to do it yourself. I won't be able to do it", he said while his eyes turned black too, and he was panting heavily. Is he going to attack me? Is he losing control like the others?

" Thanks. I understand...", I replied.

He caught me staring his dark eyes and deflected them towards the floor, "I have to go. I'll send Rose with some clothes. Make sure you tend to your wounds before she comes", saying this he left.

I've never seen Levi talking much. He always used to stick with Jared if Rose wasn't there. A stern face expression never left his face. He seemed like an army man: short hairs, an excellent muscular built, and a keen sense of surroundings. I never saw him talking much to other vampires as well, always straight to point. Come to think of it; he was the one who kidnapped me that day from my house.

I slowly went to the bathroom with the kit and washed all my small wounds with soap and water. The one inflicted by Cecily and Ria hurt the most. A burning pain felt as I applied the antibiotic on my wounds and then bandaged them. A knock on the door startled me. I just hope it's not Levi. I'm standing here naked, and the torn bloody clothes are all wet.

" I've bought your clothes. I'll hang them at the door", Rose said, and I heard a thud again. She left. When I was done with my wounds, I peeked through the door to make sure nobody is there and yanked the pink satin gown.

I slowly went to bed and laid myself down. My whole body felt like many needles have pierced through my skin at once.

****

I woke up in the middle of the night. How long was I sleeping? It was 2.30. My body felt weak and exhausted. All I had was just a single apple, and the kitchen was empty. My stomach craved food. I went towards the table to check, but all I could see were just apples. I grabbed one and ate it. The bottle was empty, and I felt very thirsty. I needed water.

Grabbing the empty bottle, I headed towards the door. I checked both sides of the hallway. It was pitch black. I couldn't see a thing. Since I've arrived here, never did I ever saw the lights being switched off, not even at night.

I remember Claude telling me once vampires mostly go on a hunt at night and rarely sleep. Only the ones who are young like Charles sleep. But still, why are lights out today. Going downstairs now is a bad idea. I don't have a torch or a phone. I don't want to fall to my death. So I turned back to my room.

A cold breeze gushed through my wrist as I entered my room. I closed all the windows. A loud shatter flabbergasted me. I turned only to find the broken splinters of the vase which was previously kept on the table.

I stood horrified at the sight. How's that possible?

If William comes to know this, I'll be shattered in as many pieces as this vase. I went towards the switch, and I heard a creaking sound of the door which was now shut.

I felt a presence behind me. Whoever it was, I could feel his breath on my neck below my ears. I was frightened by this presence. I made a run for outside but was pinned on the door. I felt a cold hand that muzzled my mouth tightly. I wanted to let out a scream, but I was unable to. I couldn't see who it was. The lights were out. He held both of my hands above my head, and his weight kept my body still. I struggled to get out of his grip, but it was in vain. Whoever it was, he was mighty. I tried to open my mouth to bite his palm, but I couldn't even move my lips due to the intense pressure. Tears formed in my eyes, and I started weeping.

He took me and laid me on the bed, and as the moonlight flashed his face, I could see who it was.

"Hello butterfly...", I heard a coarse yet familiar voice, and he released his hand from my mouth.

" Scott...", I stayed there shocked, heavily breathing.

"Don't be scared, love. I'm not here to kill you or drink your blood ...", he said while I was pinned on my back.

"Please leave me..." I cried.

"Oh sure...once we play for a while, then I'll leave you..." he smirked.

I screamed for help while he continued laughing, " Nobody would hear you... Everyones out for a feed. They won't be back by morning. "

"Please don't do this..." I cried.

I started screaming in shock and panicked as he moved his face towards mine. He slowly pulled one of my sleeves down my shoulder and started to kiss my neck—one of his hands gripping my arms while the other looped my waist. Fear and disgust filled inside my heart, and I kept screaming for help.

Suddenly he stopped kissing and asked me, "Who are you?".

I got startled by his question and confused by what he meant.

"I've never lost my restraint on human blood. Yet I have this craving to drink you dry. Your mana must be cloaked, but your scent drives me crazy. I've never felt this before...Who are you..." Scott said, ogling at my chest.

"I don't understand what you're saying. Please let me go..." I wept heavily, and I heard a loud thud from the door. I felt his weight off my body, and I stood up.

"You bastard...Keep your hands off her", it was Levi. He grabbed Scott and threw him down towards the bookshelf breaking it. Many books fell on his head, but he didn't budge. He was unaffected and smiling like a crazy person.

" Levi...my man... I'm just having a little fun. I don't want to hurt her," Scott said, getting all dirt from his shirt.

"Shut up and leave... I'll not hesitate to rip your throat...", Levi growled at him.

" Woah...Aren't you forgetting who you are talking to?" Scott said in an authoritative, arrogant tone.

"I don't care a damn if you are a prince or whatever. Leave now..." he warned him, clenching his fists. I could see his blue veins on his pale skin, which shimmered under the moonlight.

"Fine, I'll leave... I'll get even just don't forget that... Ciao, my beautiful butterfly... I'll see you around..." he shamelessly winked at me. I ignored him. I don't even want to see his sickening face.

Levi turned the lights on, and I quickly straightened my clothes.

"Are you hurt?" he inquired.

I nodded, saying no.

He quickly asked, "Are you ok?"

"Serena..?"

I didn't say anything. I was too traumatized by this. All the bad memories that I've been hiding in my heart came out as terrible reoccurrence. He came close and tried to touch my arm, but I instinctively moved back. I just wanted to be alone...

"Ok ok fine...Don't panic. I'll leave. I was just worried...Just lock the door I'll be in the mansion only. Don't worry and sleep," he said and left.

****

William's POV

We halted in the middle of the forest. Ada said we would reach by tomorrow evening. We would have saved at least one day if the witches didn't have to rest every night. Weaklings...

Both of them slept inside the tent, whereas I kept a watch outside with Ivan. He was sitting and thinking.

The way he behaved back at the palace concerned for that girl, I just couldn't take that off my mind. Has he started to like her, or is he putting a show?

The last time I sensed, he had no control over his mana. He was a ticking time bomb. But that day, during the fight with Rowan, I discerned his mana has grown powerful and has a delicate control over it. I don't know why, but I think he had got as powerful as me and has even acquired the skill to mask his mana.

I can never tell what he thinks. He is one smart, cunning bastard. I'm sure he's up to something. The way he is sitting, I am sure he is scheming out some calculations about his next hundred moves; I just have to know somehow what he is conspiring.

I couldn't let this girl out of my hands. I need to kill that bitch and her brother.

I was so lost in my thoughts. I didn't notice the faint stench. Ivan was already in a fighting stance. I went inside the tent and woke up Eva, "We've got company."

Chapter 13 – Power

William's POV

The stench became intense as they arrived closer. I could feel four manas, one of them being stronger compared to others. The crushing sound of leaves sharpened. Ivan was ready to attack Ada, and Eva stood behind us. Glowing goldish eyes were visible behind the thick vegetation.

A big grey wolf appeared with a girl riding on him. Two smaller wolves stood next to him, a brown and a smaller version of grey.The girl had brown curly hair that matched her brown cat eyes, tanned skin, and a petite physique. I felt like I've seen her before but not sure where. The scent she emitted was not of a werewolf or a vampire.

And the fact that she had faint mana resembled she was not a human as well. She got down from her wolf and stood next to him.

"Crystal? Is that you?" Eva asked in a surprise.

"Yes, Eva... I'm so happy to see you after so many years," she replied with teary eyes. It was an unexpected reunion. I remembered then where I saw her and anger fumed throughout my body.

"She is a Bloodstone witch, " Ivan growled in anger.

"Was..." she corrected, " I was a Bloodstone witch, but I left those crazy psychos a lot before the crazy massacre."

My body was burning with anger as she mentioned that bloody night. We killed everyone from their family. Not even a single person was spared. I never imagined one must have escaped after all these centuries.

"We must kill her, "I screamed at Eva. I could hear a loud growl from the grey wolf ready to attack.

" I haven't done anything wrong. I wasn't even there when the bloodshed took place. And I despised the Bloodstones, which is why I left", she convincingly said.

"I heard you eloped with some human when you came of age," Eva stated.

Why would a witch go with a human? Most of the witches are usually vowed to chastity like Ada, Eva, and Cassandra, and as far as I remember, Eva once said some of them do get married but only with their kind to keep their bloodlines pure.

"I did elope...But not with a human. That was a lie the Bloodstones came up with to prevent their humiliation that would come if everyone knew I ran with a wolf...a werewolf. I was a disgrace to them", she replied, gazing towards the grey wolf.

" You did whattttt," Eva yelled in surprise. We all were astonished. It was unheard of a witch and a werewolf being together. Witches are supposed to serve vampires right from the beginning of time. And werewolves are natural enemies of vampires, so that made the other two enemies indirectly.

"I couldn't help...He is my mate. I love him. I couldn't stay away from him... And nobody would understand our bond, so running away was the only option. We were running away and hiding for a long time. But one day we came to know the Gregors and the Reese demolished every one of them. We were so happy and genuinely grateful to you both. It's a sheer coincidence that we were fated to meet like this", she replied bowing towards us, while the grey wolf shifted to a completely naked human.

"Samvastra," Ada quickly chanted a spell which covered the exposed wolf's lower body. The other two wolves stood in their wolf form, still, alert.

"Thanks for that...." he winked at Ada and continued to talk, facing us, " I am Ryan Greyhound, Alpha of the Night Shade pack. I am indebted to both your families for destroying the Bloodstones and finally let me have my Crystal. My pack and I mean no harm to your families, and also we don't harbor any feelings of vengeance", he declared.

"We cannot trust them. They came to attack us..." I muttered. I didn't trust these dogs. Werewolves, Vampires, and Trust is some kind of a sick fantasy that is as good as big bullshit. Do they take us for some fools?

"We had to come because we sensed strong manas and vampire on our pack land. Just trust us; we don't mean any harm...", Crystal said convincingly, meeting Ivans's eyes lovingly as if he's the hero and I'm the villain...

" They speak the truth. I can sense them, and I'm not wrong ", Ada said, gazing me.

I hissed at her...Everyone has lost it. I never doubted Ada's s judgment. She was a smart and exceptionally skilled witch when it comes to psychology and mind reading. Eva and Cassandra were nothing less. Eva had good spiritual energy needed for various summoning, spells, and enchantment, whereas Cassandra excelled in healing.

" I trust them," Ivan stated his opinion.

I just couldn't believe what was happening. Werewolves and Vampires allies...

"When the time comes, we will stand by you, " Ryan said, bowing towards us and the other wolves followed.

"Fine...", I replied annoyingly.

" You can rest at our packhouse, " Ryan said with a stern expression.

"No, we're fine here. We'll be leaving by dawn anyway," Ivan replied.

" As you wish," a smile crossed Ryans' face.

"But what are you all doing here in Krasnodar so far away from home?", Crystal inquired curiously, scanning our expressions.

" We've come to get find something or rather some answers..." Ivan replied calmly.

"Oh...incase if you don't find anything and still need help, let us know. We know the area very well. Or you can go to 'feu follet' if it's just some answers you want...", Crystal replied.

" You ever heard anything about masking a human with a person's mana?" Ivan quickly asked her. Sneaky little bastard. He never misses an opportunity...

Crystal sighed and stated, talking, "Well...When I was with Blood-stones, I was too young and inexperienced. There was a rogue witch who was very old but had an immense and vast knowledge of mana. I heard our witch John talking to one of the witches of our coven once...The old witch use to mask her mana on other rogue witches to protect herself from an attack. Although how she did it is unknown.

He didn't say anything about camouflaging it on humans since they don't have mana in the first place...I don't know how much of it is true, though, because that jerk was a bloody womanizer and used to blurt things to woo the witches...".

John...That Bloody scoundrel...

" Think you can find something on the old witch, her whereabouts, anyone who knows or saw her or anything..." Ivan asked, giving her a chocolaty smile. I immediately glanced at her mate, who seemed annoyed.

"I'll try to find it... I cannot promise, but I'll look into it. It'll take time...", she smiled back hesitantly and grabbed on Ryans back who was now shifted back to his wolf form.

" We will take our leave now," the alpha declared while smiling towards the witches and me & gave a cold look towards Ivan. Ivan looked a bit surprised but smiled back at Crystal. What does he think he's doing. Can't he see that she's already taken by that muscular dog. Intense mana training had driven him a perv.

"Goodbye, Eva...It was nice to meet you and everyone", Crystal waved towards us and left with her parade.

" Ada, you've never heard of that old hag"? I asked curiously.

"Nope...Never... If she's as old as what Crystal says, she might be more than two thousand years old... And practicing Black magic... Not to mention the only person I know above two thousand is Rowan. He might know something... But that's also out of the question right now...", Ada replied.

"WE ARE NOT MEETING HIM AGAIN...I'll kill him the next time I see him," Ivan replied furiously.

"There goes our last option," I replied...Even I didn't want to see that perverted douchebag again.

"But this turn of events might be in our favor. Crystal must know something about John or Matilda...She could help us," Eva said.

"Yes...But there's one thing that must be decided now itself. What do you think if the Valacs or the other vampire families come to know about our alliance with the werewolves?", Ada questioned.

" I think we should keep it between Cassandra and us. Nobody else should know. Not even our kindred or our family," I replied, waiting for Ivan's reply.

"I agree... Ada, even my mother, shouldn't know about this. It might put them in danger. So only the four of us and Cassandra should know", Ivan replied.

" But the queen...", Ada was interrupted by Ivan, "She WAS the queen, and I AM the King...".

I was stunned, so was Eva by his choice of words that too with Ada. But Ada didn't seem surprised by the way he talked. I've never seen him being so disrespectful that also with Ada of all people. It was visible how time and power had transformed him. He sounded so authoritative and arrogant.

" I understand..." she quietly replied.

"I'm sleepy... Let's go, Ada" Eva quickly jumped in the conversation cutting the awkward situation.

Both of them went inside the tent while we stayed at guard. Tomorrow is going to be a long day...

Chapter 19 – Feu Follet

Ivan's POV

"There's nobody here. Are you sure we've come to the right spot?" I asked.

"Yes...We need to wait until the witching hour", Eva replied gazing at the moon.

I sighed. I just wanted to return back to Serena as soon as possible. The moment I saw her, the first time, I had this feeling to be with her, to protect her and cherish her and make her mine...

She was too beautiful and innocent. I want to remove her from William's clutches as soon as possible. I still feel very angry at the fact that he got her first. Luckily, that muscle-head isn't interested in her like I am, but still, she's not safe with him. I can't control my anger when I see him tormenting her.

I had asked Claude to look after her and he willingly agreed. In fact, he was more than ready. Come to think of it he too has the same look in his eye as mine. It seems he too has a soft spot for Serena. But is it love or friendship I just am not sure. He's too secretive, the reason I keep him away from my matters. William is still hot-headed softy who can't see Claude's true nature behind his jolly personality. Claude can conceal the dark side of his mana from everyone but I had once felt a hint of it after my rigorous training. I can't allow him to come in my way. Serena is mine...

I just need to push my mother for Irene and his wedding...

We stood at the base of a mountain at the lakeshore. The lake stood calm before us, enfolded by mountains on all sides, cloaked with snow-capped coniferous trees. The surface of the lake mirrored the constellations and the starlight. The sky sparkled in different hues of blue, which reflected in the silver moonlight.

Almost an hour was left until the spirit appear. Ada sat with Eva. Their eyes seemed bewitched at the enchanting sight. I gazed at

William, who seemed very restless. Something was bothering him. I felt a commotion in his mana, a weird disturbance, from a few minutes. His breathing pattern was also slightly distorted. He walked in circles gripping his hair grinning his teeth.

Suddenly, I felt my heartbeats sped up. Uneasiness felt throughout my body. My body trembled in anger - a fit of anger; I had no idea why. There's no reason why I would feel it now. Maybe it's because of this place. I gazed at Eva and Ada. Both appeared to stare at William. However, they didn't seem angry or in pain themselves. It was just the two of us who suffered. My eyes turned toward William, who was heavily panting. He had jet black eyes. He was pacing in circles in anxiety.

"What's wrong with you both?", Ada asked.

"I am feeling nervous and angry for some reason... Something's not right..." William replied, uprooting a tree in rage. I felt the same. My heartbeat was speeding rapidly as restlessness rose.

"I feel the same," I replied as I tried scanning for manas. I couldn't find any. We weren't under attack. So what's this feeling.

"You think it's the spirit?" Ada asked Eva.

"I don't think so. She's never known to hurt any supernatural beings irrespective of their nature or intentions", Eva replied.

'Sirius alpezo'

Ada cast a spell, but I still felt the discomfort. The spell was ineffective. My eyes gazed at William, who caused havoc in the woods. A part of the forest was cleared with all the fallen lumber.

My heart was pounding in my chest, trying to escape from my body. My mana felt something more than outrage and suffering- It was Fear...

****

After a few minutes, I felt better. My heart calmed down, and my mana got stable, so did William's.

"Just what was that all about," Eva asked.

"I have no idea," Ada replied.

" We need to leave soon. I'm worried about Charles", William replied while still heavily panting.

"Yes...Its time now. She'll come any moment," Eva replied.

Suddenly there was an eerie silence. The wind stopped gushing. My eyes focused on the lake surface as I saw it forming ripples. White and turquoise light glowed, and out came a gorgeous woman in a long silver silky dress. Her long white lustrous hair flowed all the way till her legs. Her pale skin glistened in the moonlight. A beautiful sapphire studded locket around her delicate neck caught my attention while her purple eyes gazed us with curiosity. William cleared his throat and passed me an evil smirk. He caught me checking her out but it wasn't something I could have controlled. Her beauty was mesmerizing. He was still gaping me and had a smug look on his face as though he's mocking me. I don't care whatever he thought. It was not my problem that he wasn't that interested in beautiful females. I took my sweet time gazing at the sexy water goddess.

Eva and Ada quickly bowed to her.

"Son of Cornelius. I didn't hope to see you again after our last rendezvous and daughters of Aradia, what brings you here? You have bought the Reese King as well."

Again????... William has been here previously??? What did he want to know? Was it about Emma...I need to find out. I looked at William who was expressionless whereas Eva seemed flustered as my eyes met her. They're caught... She stole her gaze away from mine and Ada's and looked at the spirit, "O spirit of the feu follet, we wish you to heed us for we want to know some answers."

"I see...Seeing the two of them coming, it must be something significant. However, the last time you were here Eva your spiritual power lasted only for a minute. Are you sure this time you can keep up with me?" the spirit asked.

Eva too came here. She just confirmed. Ada wouldn't miss telling me these details. Maybe they kept it a secret. Too bad I got to know. But for what reason...Now I am really curious.

"Yes...We can start", Eva replied.

The spirit moved her hands as though she was dancing on the small waves that were formed circling her. Her hands flawlessly grazed over the tides as if they were an extension of her arms. The water took the form of a small bowl-like structure as she started with her spells. She removed the sapphire pendant and placed it in the bowl. Suddenly a white light flashed through it. I instantly shut my eyes in response. For a few seconds, it felt like my eyes are blinded. I blinked them slowly and I was shocked to see what was standing in front of me.

"No wa...", was all that left my mouth as I quickly managed to get a grip on my tongue. A grotesque old woman stood in front of me. She had long white grime hair, a few of its strands covered her purple eyes. Her skin looked wrinkled and had a pale white colorless pall to it. As she was chanting, I saw her black serrated rotten teeth beneath her vulturous nose. Her nails were like long sharp claws filled with dark disgusting gunk. The only thing that didn't change was her purple eyes.

I realized the mocking grin which William had a few minutes ago. He knew about her true form. My eyes stared his, which were glued to the spirit, and his face seemed amused at my horrified reaction.

Eva started connecting the spirit. Her eyes turned white so did her hair. A white light connected her with the spirit as she levitated in the air. I felt a shift in mana. Eva was rapidly losing all her mana while the old hag gaining the same.

"What do you want to know?", the old spirit asked in her raspy voice.

"We need to know about a human, Serena Rosewood. How she has two manas that too being a human? How to remove them?"

"Serena Rosewood an ordinary human but not ordinary at the same time. She has two manas at present. One of them placed by the Bloodstone wizard John, rightful heir to the Queen of the witches - Aradia. It was placed by a treizeouzz magic, a very ancient dark magic that takes a span of thirteen years to complete. It can be used to mask a supernatural being with another person mana. John masked his twin sister Matilda's mana on the human. The other mana which the human has is it's her own. Being a human she has her own mana is something that had never ever occurred which makes her very special. Although she has no powers. Her own mana cannot be withdrawn from her until her death. To remove the other dark mana, she must drink the blood of the two 'Guardians', the spirit said.

"What do you mean by Guardians?", Eva asked.

"Guardians are her the protectors. A bond will be formed between them soon which I cannot see now. They would feel everything that she feels ", the spirit replies.

" Who are the Guardians?"

" My spirit doesn't allow me to disclose anything more about them as it is destiny that would unveil the fate that lies ahead. But as per the prophecy, the guardians will bear the power of the moon", the spirit replied.

"Power of moons? Do you mean werewo..."

Before completing her sentence Eva collapsed and the old hag disappeared. William rushed towards Eva and made her drink something that he removed from his pocket. Eva had very faint mana, which slowly vitalized as she drank the complete potion.

" Damn....", William growled in frustration.

"I'm sorry, I couldn't hold any longer", Eva apologized teary-eyed.

"It's ok. I'm glad at least we got something", William said affectionately.

"John is from Aradia's bloodline. I can't believe it...", Ada screamed in surprise.

"I know I was equally shocked...", Eva whispered.

"Who is Aradia?", I asked.

"She is believed to be the Queen of witches in ancient legends. Nobody had ever believed it to be true since there was no record for the tales. But for John being the heir it means Matilda is too...", Ada replied.

" Are you too as well? She referred you as daughters of Aradia?", I asked.

"No...that was a generalized title that she gives to all witches", Ada explained.

"How do we get the guardian's blood now. We don't even know for sure if they're werewolves or something else", William growled in anger and frustration.

"Why don't we come here again and ask next time", I asked.

"She helps a particular person only once a century...We can't wait for another hundred years", Eva replied.

"The next time we can bring Cassandra or Margaret", I stated.

"Cassandra cannot. She needs to wait at least 10 more years now", Eva replied. It means Cassandra was here 90 years ago with William. The reason why she hasn't come this time. I knew something was off when she sent Eva.

"Margaret's spiritual powers won't last for more than a few seconds. The spirit is too powerful for her and the other witches are very young and weak. I also cannot come unless my curse is lifted", Ada replied gazing the ground. She seemed very furious. Matilda placed a curse on Ada that didn't allow her to communicate any spirits. The reason is still unknown and Ada always ignores whenever this topic comes up.

"Crystal...?", Eva whispered but I knew it was a wrong option at least at this point of time.

"No, we still don't trust her completely...Let's wait until she approaches us with whatever information she gets about the old witch. Then we can think...", I replied.

"Ok. Lets first leave from here. I need to see Charles. We still don't know what happened to us some time ago. I am feeling very paranoid. Let's leave for the castle now....", William said as we left.

Chapter 15 - Nobody

Cassandra's POV

The rays sheathed my skin like a warm cloak. My eyes were unable to bear the intense sun. The radiant glow made it difficult for me to open my eyes. I kept blinking them for a few seconds and finally gazed at the clear sky.

It feels so good to be in sunlight again. Everything seemed peaceful around. Luckily there was no crisis while I was away.

The one week felt like one long month. Though I enjoyed my me-time after so many years, I still missed Eva. I'm just eager to tell her all the extraordinary things I found in those rare ancient books.

I wished we should have read them before. I'm happy those evil siblings left the 'Book of Aradia' behind. How did they even get their hands on one of the books of Queen of the Witches? I want to read the other two books of this trilogy...Who knows where they must be...

My joints ached all over due to the cramped position I sat in the library. Finally, I'll have something other than instant cup noodles. My body was screaming for a relaxing bath.

I couldn't feel many manas from the mansion. It seems they haven't reached yet. They were supposed to come today...

Suddenly my eyes went to my deserted garden. My breath was caught in my throat. I was dumbfounded by the sight that met my eyes. The piece of land where my garden stood resembled a spooky graveyard. All my flowers stood like burnt carcasses. I tried to touch one of my lilies but it withered away in the air. Waves of anger rushed through my blood and I felt my temper rising with my blood boiling in my veins.

"Cecily..."

"Cecily...Where the hell are you?"

I screamed at the top of my lungs, seething in rage, calling her out, but she didn't come. My heart was beating rapidly inside my chest. I gazed at the main door, and I saw Anna coming out.

"Everyone's out at this moment. They have gone for a feed...", she replied.

"May I know where is my garden...", I asked her furiously.

"What..." she seemed confused like I've lost my mind and stared at me with a blank expression.

"Do you call this thing a garden......This deserted barren piece of land? I clearly warned her to water them. But look at them...", I was nearly on the verge of a mental breakdown. Anger and despair filled my heart, seeing the sight of the arid ground.

"I had no idea..." she said in a defensive tone.

"You had no idea, you say?... You do have eyes, don't you?... Do you even realize how long it takes them to grow? And what if there is a crisis. I wouldn't be able to heal you and perform some crucial enchantments without my herbs...You do realize that, don't you...", I lashed out in rage. At this point of time, nothing she said was going to calm me. I was losing my patience and my anger got the best of me...

"I'm sorry," she apologized gazing down.

"Where is Martha? Martha....", I called out for Martha. I dint expected she would ever forget my plants, even though she was not told to look after them.

"Uh...em...All humans are on leave", she replied.

"What!!!!"

"Eh...em...Cecily asked them to leave for one week since you weren't coming out of the library ", she whispered with stammering words.

"Is she out of her mind...Oh god...I don't know what I'll do now...L eave... Just leave before I lose myself", I frowned and the next second she vanished with her supernatural speed. I felt strong mana from the west speedily coming towards me. It was him...Where did he go when I had him to look after Serena.

I gazed at the woods. He came walking in his button-loose white shirt casually grazing tunneling his fingers through his chocolaty brown hair.

"Hi, Cassie... Who got you fumed today?", Claude asked. Before I could answer I felt more manas coming from the south. Both of us gazed in that direction.

"They've come...", I whispered.

William was the first to appear. He looked dreadful with his messed up hair and clothes tainted in the dirt. His expression looked extremely worried and tensed. I wonder what happened...

"Where's Charles? Is everything ok here?", he asked heavily panting.

"Yes, he's fine...I just had a look at him. He was busy painting in his room. What happen? ", I asked.

He let a sigh of relief and immediately ran inside towards Charles' room. I stood there stunned with Claude. Ivan and Eva entered the mansion stood next to us.

"My goodness...What's with our garden", Eva exclaimed in shock. She appeared very wearied, completely drained of mana and worn out as Ivan slowly let her down from his arms.

"Don't ask. Already I'm out of my mind...What's with William? Let's go in", I said as we all followed William. We stood in the hall only to find him lying on the couch with a bag of blood.

"What happened there", I asked curiously.

"I thought Charles was in danger. When we went there before we met the spirit, I felt a very uneasy feeling. I felt very restless along with rage and fear. I cannot explain...It was as if someone close to me needs my help as if someone is in danger...I just don't understand why...", William replied...

"But how...Charles is absolutely fine", I mumbled in surprised.

"I don't know. I just don't know...", William looked frustrated and demented. Whatever he said were signs of the mate bond...

"I too felt the same, at the same time...", Ivan stated.

"Whattttt!!! That can't be true", I was shocked. How's this possible. No there must be some mistake.

"Were you attacked?", I asked to confirm my doubts.

"No, we weren't. We all tried to sense any manas, there was none. But what happen? Why are you so shocked", Eva replied, her voice laced with confusion and worry.

I was totally shocked by what I was hearing. Charles had been attacked once by a rogue, a century back while William was away, but that time he didn't feel Charles' pain. Luckily, Claude was there to save him. So this was definitely not the blood-bond. Charles was not in danger as well and William still felt the bond...And Ivan too, that too at the same time...Maybe it's not Charles but someone else. But still, it can't be a mate bond...Both cannot have the same mate...It must be something else.

"This is a kind of bonding. And it's not about Charles and its not even blood-bonding since Ivan felt it as well. Usually mates have such bonding but both of them felt the same at the same time, so I don't think this is mate-bonding...", I replied. Everything was so damn confusing. Both of them can't have the same mate. Its something else..."What did the spirit tell?"

"John & Matilda are from Aradia's bloodline. She is real...Not a myth", Eva spoke. My eyes widened in horror.

"Whattt!!!!", was all I could say. My brain was too weak to process all the information. My heartbeats rose as I managed to get a seat next to William and continued, "I cannot believe this. I found a book written by Aradia. It was the one which we sacked after the Bloodstones were killed. There's no mention of her heirs of any sort..."

"No way...That's great...Anyways, the spirit also said Serena is a special human and Matilda's mana had been placed on her by a 'treizeouzz' spell which can only be removed if she drinks the blood of her two 'Guardians' who apparently have the power of the moon", Eva stated.

"Who are the Guardians?", I asked.

"That's all we were able to find out", Eva sighed as she sat on the dining table and got a glass of water.

"We are stuck again... Anyways let's think about this tomorrow. We need a break now...I'm totally exhausted from his long journey. Where's Serena? I want to see her before I leave", Ivan asked while his eyes surveyed the room. I totally forgot to check on her...

"Come to think of it. Where is she Claude?" , I asked while he was already sniffing for her scent at a room next to the kitchen.

"The strong smell...She's in that room. What she's doing there? Serena come out...It's me, Claude...Serena", he called her out. The door opened slowly and her eyes landed on Claude. We stood there shocked at her sight. She came running out of the room with her messed up hair. The right side of her dress was torn from her neckline till her midriff. She held the frayed shreds of that garment close to her chest, preventing the exposure. As she came close, a red mark of fingers was visible on her pale cheek. There were many wounds and dark bruises on her bare skin. She was heavily crying as she saw us and fell unconscious into Claude's arms. We all stood stunned, unable to understand what was going on. My legs refused to move in shock at her sight while Claude immediately removed his shirt and covered her.

I felt an elevation in his mana. Rage and Fury filled mana flooded out of his body. His mana rose to an extent that we could physically feel it. All the windows shattered due to his immensely powerful mana which was still rising. I had never ever felt any mana like this in my whole life. It was dark, scary, ruthless. All of us stepped away from him including Ivan and William. They were too overwhelmed by that tremendous energy oozing out of him. My eyes gazed his pitch-black eyes which screamed - Death .

"Who did this?" he roared in anger. Everyone took a few more steps back. His voice was too intimidating. Serena laid there still bleeding and unconscious cocooned in his overprotective massive arms. He was furious and agitated but still, his grip on her was delicate.

"Claude, calm down...", William took a step towards him but he growled at him angrily with his fangs while tightening his grip on her. William had to step back quickly. His instincts told that if we pissed him further, it would be the end of us. He was astounded at Claude's sudden change. On the other hand, Ivan was completely focused on him. He didn't seem shocked or surprised by Claude.

I took a step forward and said, "Claude, listen to me...You need to calm down. She is still bleeding and you may hurt her unknowingly. I need to save her as much as you want to. Trust me...You need to control yourself". He didn't growl back at me and his breathing calmed down so did his anger. He closed his black eyes and opened back those brown eyes which again in an instant turned blood-red after seeing Serena. But his mana was controlled.

He lifted her carefully and unleashed his wrath while his eyes glowed red, "Nobody comes close...except Cassandra..."

"Nobody..."

Chapter 16 - Dark

Claude's POV

"What do you mean you don't have any herbs left?", I asked her, controlling my anger.

"There was a little incident while I was locked in my library and my garden is dead which is the reason I was fuming in the morning. But don't worry I have something else...", she answered.

"Cassandra, please do something fast. I can't watch her like this", I was at the brink of losing my sanity. I was really depressed as well as furious seeing Serena's condition. She laid there inert soaked in blood. Her milky white skin had wounds with dark purple bruises all over her body. Her breathing was ragged and her body was cold almost lifeless. It looked frail and malnourished. The big wound on her abdomen and her arm caught my attention. It was as if someone had stabbed her with a sharp object. Her sweet honey-like scent was mixed with a wood-like one. It didn't belong to anyone from the Gregors. I've been here for many centuries and I know very well how everyone smelled. I got close to her neck to sniff it, a strange faint scent confirmed my doubts which trailed her cheeks, neck, and chest - It belonged to a male.

I felt immense pain in my heart looking at her. I swear I won't leave the bastard who did this. I held her soft hands in mine and waited for Cassandra to get over with her spell.

'kzsaksharu sarino boka ze palac ni saro ni saro ni saro'

A white light glowed from Serena's body. I couldn't see a thing that was happening while Cassandra continued chanting something weird. A few minutes later she collapsed while Serena still laid un-conscious. The wounds were still there. She was still in pain.

"What was that? She is not healed...", I asked.

"I had used a very ancient spell on her. She didn't heal because I was not that powerful but I managed to take away all her pain and catalyzed her healing. She wouldn't feel any sort of physical pain and would wake up after two days completely healed".

I let out a sigh of relief.

"Can you leave for a moment. I need to clean her wounds and get her changed", she said.

"Alright. I'll wait outside the door", I said and left the room.

I didn't want to leave. I didn't trust anybody here. It was all my fault. I shouldn't have left her here alone. She must be so scared. It's all my fault. I can never forgive myself for this...

I waited for Cassandra to be done. As soon as she was done, I hurriedly went inside. All her body was wrapped in bandages. Her breathing was very slow and her heartbeats were feeble. Grief filled my heart with pure rage, for whoever was responsible for this.

"I need some answers. Let's go down", I said while Cassandra followed me.

As soon as my eyes met everyone else's, I could see fear and horror creeping over their faces. I was not going to leave any one of them or whoever was responsible for my love's condition. As I was stepping downstairs, everyone stood alarmed posed themselves in a fighting stance, and at the same time shifted away from the staircase, away from me.

By this time, I could see everyone returned including Levi. "Levi, I said you to protect her no matter what. What the hell happened here ?" I snapped at him.

"It was Cecily...She invited some of her friends and all of them tortured Serena", Levi replied shaking in fear.

"Cecily...", I screamed her name and lunged at her. I lifted her through her throat. She shrieked for air and dug her nails into my skin attempting to free herself. It was all in vain. Pathetic weaklings. Not a single person here was as strong as me. Neither William nor Ivan or the witches. I felt William and Ivan pulling me away from her trying to restrain me while I was draining the life out of her.

"If you don't want Serena to be terrified of you - 'the real you', Release her ", Ivan interrupted. It was only him who had ever got a glimpse of my true strength, the beast inside me. I noticed he had a thing for Serena but I knew it was not more than lust for the playboy he was. As if I was ever going to let him have her. But I didn't want Serena to see my dark side as well. I wanted to take things slow and win her heart after all she was the reason I got...

I was lost in my train of thoughts and didn't realize when my grip on her neck loosened and almost everyone present there held me back away from her.

"I was just following our King's orders", she replied as she collapsed on the floor while still coughing.

I stared at William who looked angry as well as disappointed, "Claude why?"

"Because I love her dammit...The day when I saw her, I wanted her more than anything else and I will do anything for her...", I snapped ignoring a hundred pairs of black eyes surrounding me. I just don't care now for as long as it's clear to everyone that she belongs to me.Only me. And anyone who dares to look at her will meet a very painful gruesome death.

"But my parent's death...my whole family...it wa...", William convincingly said while I interrupted him, "Will, when are you going to understand. It was not her...It was that bitch, Matilda. Serena is just innocent and used by those evil siblings who were responsible for your parent's death. Not her. You are blinded by your anger. Just snap out of it. Until now I had kept quiet by the way you treated her just because I wanted you to realize your mistake. I felt so furious every time I saw you hurting her but I still kept quiet just for the sake of our friendship. If you still harbor any ill-will or hatred towards her, I'll have to go against you or anyone that comes in my way...".

" Claude....", William whispered in a sorrowful voice. He was clearly upset and shattered by my harsh words. So was I, but I couldn't bear seeing my love in any more pain.

"She stays with me now in my room. And nobody lays a hand on her...", I growled angrily.

"Very well...If that's what you wish..." William replied. He was still upset but he agreed. I am sure he'll understand in some time...

I faced Levi and the others who were ready to leave the hall trying to escape from me, "I AM NOT DONE YET...WHO TOUCHED HER? " Everyone stood stunned while I felt the dark side of my mana taking over slowly.

"What do you mean?" Cassandra asked gazing me.

"She had torn clothes and I could smell a male scent all over her...Who touched her?" I asked angrily while everyone took a step back. I faced Levi, " I'll not repeat it...Levi speak".

"It was the Draken prince...Scott Draken. He..he.. attempted to r... r...".

"Tell me...", I bursted in anger. Everyone was terrified and gaped at each other...

"He attempted to rape her but I managed to save her from him and made him leave", Levi replied.

"NO..." was all that came out of my mouth while William and Ivan looked angry. Eva covered her mouth in shock whereas Cassandra stood in shock with her widened eyes.

This was the limit. My blood was literally boiling in my veins in wrath. I let out a loud growl in anger which shook everyone and punched the table which broke into pieces. All I could see was re d....and blood..., "That son of a bitch, I'll kill him."

"Claude...No...Calm down.."

"Claude..."

"No Claude....."

I heard voices calling me but I was unable to interpret...my vision was blurred...I lost my control...I threw the chairs and whatever that was coming in my way. I smashed a wall in front of me which created a huge hole in it and eventually, it completely crumbled. The debris was all over the place and on me as I continued my rampage. I tried to restrain myself so as to avoid the bloodbath... But slowly, I felt my sanity slipping out of me...

Suddenly, I heard a voice.......

'Claude'

'Claude Calm down...'

'Claude'

I heard a sensual sweet voice. It had a soothing effect on me. It was my love...my Serena...

I quickly calmed down and my eyes searched for her but I didn't see her except for the frightened fanged weaklings encircling me.

"Control yourself, Claude...It was not Serena. It was just a spell. She's still laying peacefully in your room", Cassandra said. I hissed at her for tricking me but I was equally thankful that she saved me from turning into a rogue.

"Claude, they are very powerful. Don't forget he's a pureblood. Let's handle it some other way", Cassandra convincingly said. She sounded worried even though she didn't like me much.

"Handle what dammit...She was tortured and that bastard he...he tried to...And worst part of it, I left her alone. I should have been here with her but I left her leaving alone to face all this torment...", I broke down in anger.

"Calm down Claude. She'll be ok. And we are lucky she remained unharmed. Thanks to Levi..." Eva said turning to me. Her soft words comforted me. I was indebted to Levi. Thankfully I asked him to guard her.

"But she's still in danger. I'm still shocked why they haven't come here yet seeking her" Ivan interrupted. As always he was the cunning smarty who always study a situation from all angles maintaining his calm demeanor.

"They wouldn't...Scott is my best friend. He had given me his word he wouldn't tell anyone. And he had wiped everyone's memories that she's our prisoner and made them believe that she's a normal human maid. He even manipulated his sister Scarlett's memories", Cecily spoke.

"You foolish woman. There were prisoners in the dungeon, our secrets, our documents everything you left vulnerable. Do you even realize how they could have misused it against us? Already they are keen to remove all royals so that they can dominate everyone and rule", Cassandra spatted on her.

"Do you even realize Cecily you have risked us all by your imprudence. If the council would have known they would have eliminated us all labeling us traitors" William yelled at her. However, it was not because of my Serena but for his family, kindred, and of course for me. Even though he was hot-headed, he was a softy inside. He cared a lot for his family and kindred. He was extremely loyal which is why I respected him.

" I'm sorry. But trust me Scott won't tell anyone I assure you", Cecily assured.

" He better not...Else we need to be prepared for war..." Ivan stated.

I didn't expect this coming from Ivan. Why would he fight for my love? Does he love her as well? Or he has some hidden motives? What are his true intentions?

Chapter 17 – Turmoil

For all my readers, kindly read this chapter and the next bloodlines carefully if you don't wanna get confused.

Claude's POV

"I can't believe this. William, it's too risky...And Ivan you too?" Cassandra gasped sitting on the couch. Even I was astounded at these turn of events. We couldn't ever be 'friends' with wolves. I don't understand how these two kings agreed. They had put everyone in danger with their decision. I had no intention to form any sort of alliance with those wild dogs. I just wanted my love to be safe.

"I was against it initially. But currently, Crystal's the only beneficial lead we have and we keep it only between us", William said. His expression was calm while his gaze directed toward rubble caused by me.

"But still if the Valacs or the Councill comes to know that we have 'befriended' the wolves, we are doomed", Cassandra argued. It was evident she was not so happy with the outcome of their visit.

"We'll handle it somehow. And I think our first priorities should be getting our moonstones back. If we get back our abilities, we can defend ourselves", blurted the power-hungry bastard. Since Emma left, he underwent rigorous training to keep his mana under control. To think that he became as powerful as William in these past few centuries has surprised me. I can sense his mana craving for more power, he'll get by those stones.

"Very well...But still..."

"Cassandra, don't worry...", William assured her which amazed me. But I trust his instincts, so I gave in. There were many other things bothering me at this moment - Red Ridge, Irene, Scott, the council, that son-of-bitch Rowan...He had left but I know he'll come back for my Serena. He's smelled her irresistible scent and unlike Scott he's not a pureblood. Levi was lucky to be unscathed. Had he used his real power, Levi would be no more and my Serena...NO...NO...I'm glad I asked Levi to protect her.

"Claude"

"Helllo....."

"Claude"

I was distracted in my own thoughts, I didn't catch a word they were saying. I just gazed them while they called my names, "Sorry, I zoned off....".

"Come to think of it, where did you take off Claude leaving your 'love' alone" Ivan asked narrowing his eyes towards me in suspicion. It was because of him, his family that I had to leave my love and she had to face the humiliation...Anger fumed off me as I observed his smirk, his expressions, his face...a replica of his cunning mother and his crazy sister....

"Because your mother called for me", my words spurted out with fury. He was astonished and confused so was everyone else...

"What why?", he asked.

I regained my control and inhaled a deep breath before facing Ivan and continued, "There are so many things going on I just don't know where to start...Your sister had totally lost it. She wants to MARRY ME...I cannot marry her. I never loved Irene and never agreed to this. But still, she's forcing me and threatening me that she'll end her life. She even attempted to commit suicide while I was there".

"No...she didn't" , Ivan yelled in shock.

"Yes, she did...Now she's fine. Somehow I managed to calm her. You need to do something. She's slowly losing her sanity and on the brink of becoming a rogue"

"I'll talk to her" Ivan was lost in his own thoughts and so was everyone else seeing this mountain of problems coming one after another. But the thing I'm about to say would just drive them crazy. I don't know what future holds for us but its better so just get over it as soon as possible , "And there's one more thing - Zephyr is back", I finally said it.

"Whattt..."

"No way..."

"I don't believe this...".

"Did I hear correct? Are you talking about Zephyr Valac? " Eva asked as if she didn't believe what she just heard. Everyone stood stunned, widened their eyes towards me.

"Yes...He is back."

"That's crazy. After being hidden for so many centuries. Where was he?" Cassandra asked.

" I have no idea. Some people say he was dead, some said he was still in Red Ridge in disguise which I don't believe to be true, some said he stayed all his life among humans. But nobody has any idea not even Vincent or the other Valacs. We don't even know how he looks" I replied.

"Where is he now?"

"Currently, he's with the council. They don't want anyone to meet him, not even the Valacs except Felicia. He'll soon make his appearance, most probably at 'Blacksun' fest. I think it's because of this everyone has went crazy. Currently, there's a turmoil going in Red Ridge. Vincent won't give up his throne at any cost."

"Why after so many years? He could have come before as well...Why now?"

"I don't know...Nobody knows.."

****

"I don't know...Nobody knows.."

****

Chapter 18 - Symbol

Serena's POV

I felt a tingling sensation all over my body. It was wet and soft as though someone is licking me. My throat was dry and my head felt heavy. I tried to lift my arm but I couldn't. I mustered all my strength to move but I couldn't. My breath escaped my lungs and exhaustion took over. Whatever it was, I felt gross and disgusted. I just wanted to get away from it. I slowly opened my eyes to see a fat woman with short blonde-peppered hair sponging my feet. My sight was clouded. I could only see her back since she was facing my legs.

"You're awake... Please calm down miss, I was just sponging you. You'll be fine in some time. I'll bring your dinner".

It was Martha. She left smiling at me. I don't remember how I ended here. The last thing I remember is Cecily slapping and kicking me for some reason before she threw me in the janitor room knocking me unconscious. I strained my memory but nothing came up. My eyes scanned the room and realization struck me, it was not William's. A grey couch laid on the left of my bed. The walls had greyish colored tiles that matched the velvety grey sheets and pillows I laid in. It had a masculine touch. Unlike William's room, it had maple flooring which increased the warmth of the room. My eyes directed towards the right side of the room which had a similar setup of stereos and consoles like those in Charles'. Claude...That was the only person it could be...Was it Claude's room? Did he come back? My heart jolted in happiness and his presence confirmed it...

"Serena...."

The door bursted open and Claude walked in. The moment my eyes met his, my sight got blurred with unshed tears. Wet, hot of tears streamed out from my eyes trailing down through my cheeks as I managed myself to sit. Claude came running towards me and hugged me.

"Ssshhh...It's ok...I'm here now...I'll never leave you alone" he said tightening his grip on me. The warmth of his body felt so cozy, so comforting. Unconsciously, my fingers gripped his shirt and I dug my face in his massive chest and cried my heart out. I couldn't bring myself to say what happened while he was gone.

Cecily

the dart-game

Scott...

My sobs turned into heavy wails as those memories with Scott became clear in my mind.

"He...he..". My voice was choked in my throat. I tried to speak but I was breathless and all that left my mouth were sobs.

"Don't say anything...Ssshhhh....I'm here with you...I won't let anyone touch you..." he gripped me even tighter and I melted in his arms forgetting everything. We stayed in the same position for a few minutes and I steadied myself and he released his grip on me. The moment I realized we were not alone in the room, that too in this nearly intimate moment, I backed off and covered myself with the sheet. Eva and Cassandra were here the whole time along with William.

"She's completely fine now. No wounds, no scratches or bruises. Only weakness. She needs to eat something and rest..." Cassandra said facing Claude and gave me a serious expression while Eva smiled at me.

"But before she does, I have to ask her something" Eva faced him and asked as if she's asking for his permission and he nodded.

"Serena, how old were you when you were adopted?"

"Six"

"How old are you now"

"I turned 19 last month"

"That explains...thirteen years she was with them..." she continued facing the others.

" Can you remember if there was any day in your life when you were alone? I mean when your aunt Jasmine left you alone for a day or few, like you didn't see her", she asked narrowing her eyes.

Now that I think of it, I've always been a shy and introverted child. I used to get sick easily and was very weak all throughout my childhood. So Jasmine never ever left me alone. No late-night parties, no sleepovers, no school trips, not even when I grew up. For all trips, she used to get me a letter for the principal. When I grew up, I had no best friend or a close friend in girls with whom I can have a sleepover. Jeremy was the only 'friend' I had who was not even close to that title in reality. Jasmine herself never ever went to her own friends or relatives. She was always there for me...always...There was never a single day I didn't saw her...Except for the day she left...

"Never...She never left me alone...Except for the last time I saw her", I said with a shaky voice. Was Jasmine really evil as these people think? Was I living my whole life as a lie...Did she trick me all these years...All these question were storming in my head one after other.

"I knew it. She completed her spell and patiently waited thirteen years to get it done" Eva looked at everyone and declared.

"But why...when we already know the way to remove it. Don't you think it was too much hassle for her even if it meant a distraction" William asked with his composed expression? Something was changed in him. He was no more angry short-tempered beast like always but looked calm and composed.

"I think I know...", Cassandra replied drawing everyone's attention, "As the spirit of feu follet said, her mana would be taken off only when she drinks the blood of her guardians which we don't know who they are. As per the book of Aradia, if a human drinks blood from a supernatural, she gets a share of their life force. Now the question is, still, why Matilda went to such lengths to do this. I think it because along with Serena she wanted to know the identity of the two guardians. She might need the guardians and Serena as well for her evil plans but there was no way for her to know the identity of the guardians, not even with help of feu follet. Hence she placed her mana on Serena knowing that we would somehow get it removed..."

"So her leaving and letting Serena get captured now of all times is something she did purposely?" I asked.

"Yes..."

"Cunning..., yet smart move"

"So do we remove the mana or no? Does it even benefit us?" William questioned.

"Well, we need to remove it because Serena might be our key to get moonstones and we need her in her purest forms at that time, and in fact, it's better that we find those guardians soon because they would always sense her in danger and help her."

"Anyways it's late. Let's discuss it tomorrow. Let her sleep" Claude said.

Everyone left except Claude. Why is he not leaving? It is his room technically. Is he planning to sleep here? My heartbeat skyrocketed at a speed I could literally feel it throbbing in my chest. Shutting the door he leaned towards me and my body reactively went near the edge of the bed. Tunneling his fingers through his brownish-black hair he walked near the other table and lifted the tray.

"You need to eat before you sleep", he said.

"Why did you close the door?"

"Like I said I'm not leaving you alone from here on. This will be your room now on" he replied looking straight into my eye. Sub-consciously, my eyes gazed at the bed, the only bed in this room and nervousness crept over me.

Sensing my uneasiness he ruffled my hair and said, "Don't worry, I'll take the couch". He smiled at me, gently poked my forehead, and left for the couch. My fingers instinctively brushed my forehead where he just tapped me and a smile broke on my face.

I trusted him he won't do anything to me. It's just I am not so comfortable with a man touching me. Claude was the first-ever male who got so close to me. I quickly gulped the chicken-noodle soup. The heat surged throughout my body as those noodles slurped down my throat.

I was so engrossed in finishing it, I completely ignored the pair of brown eyes watching me. His face didn't have his usual cheerfulness but a tender smile. It was as if I'm not with playful, funny Claude but a kind, composed, and compassionate man. I couldn't sleep for the whole night. His eyes never left mine until darkness consumed me.

***

N^o Don't please don't

Help me... Somebody...

Serena

" Serena wake up..." Claude was fanning over me. I embraced him tightly.

"It was just a nightmare. Calm down..." I didn't want to leave him. Those people would come for me again. I clenched my arms tightly around his neck.

"Ehm...Serena..." I realized he's undressed and instantly unclasped him. I could feel the heat in my cheeks as my eyes saw his muscular body. He had nothing but a towel around his waist. A few drops of water trickled from his wet hair on my face as he towered over me.

"Sorry" was all that left from my mouth. He smiled at me and walked towards the closet. I tore my eyes away from the sight giving him the privacy he needed.

"The maid had filled the right side closet with few clothes and the bathroom with toiletries. Take your time and come down. I'll get your breakfast ready. See ya..." he said while buttoning his shirt and walked towards me. My heart skipped a beat as he brushed his lips on my forehead. My heart froze and so my body. I couldn't feel my arms and my eyes never left the door as he left the room.

What was this feeling? As if time had stopped around me. All I could hear were my own heartbeats nothing else. It was as if someone is tickling my stomach and my whole body was heating. I ran to the washroom and stripped myself in front of the mirror. The bruises we're no longer there. My hand went unconsciously tapped my forehead and my lips parted into a smile.

The shelf was filled with shampoos, soaps, scrubs, and numerous creams in lavender, Jasmine, sandalwood, and many other scents. I filled the tub with hot water and poured the strawberry colored bottle in it.

I draped a towel and selected a plain yellow short dress. It had criss-cross straps that were kinda cute.

As I went down, I could see Cassandra and Eva having breakfast whereas William was holding a glass of wine, blood-wine. The moment I came down, Claude pulled a chair for me and I joined them.

"Bon Appétit", he placed smoked salmon and blink with a french toast in cream and eggs. It smelled heavenly and tasted delicious. I saw Eva who smiled at me whereas Cassandra was totally immersed in a book. William caught my stare and I immediately moved my eyes at my plate. Claude also joined me eating eggs and caviar.

" Let's go for a walk," he said after he was done. I looked at William for approval but he seemed unfazed. Before I could say anything, Claude dragged me towards the garden, "Don't worry. He won't mind"

I kept a distance while walking next to him. It was my first time here in this garden. I always saw it from the balcony. The fountain stood in front of the main gate which had small wildflowers at its base. There was supposed to be a garden on my left but it was all barren. I wonder what happens.

"Are you ok?" he asked.

"Yes. I was just looking at the garden but its..."

"Ya, I know. Cassie sure did a number on Cecily for this" he laughed.

"Uhm...Why do you eat? I mean how can you eat food while other vampires don't?

" Well...My mother was a human. Though I am a full vampire by blood like my father still, I can feel the taste and aroma of food as well as heat and cold on my skin. Other vampires too can eat human food but it's tasteless and odorless to them. They can only taste blood" he replied gazing at the forest. That explains why his body is so warm even though he is a vampire.

"Your parents?"

"They aren't alive" he answered.

"I'm sorry"

He smiled at me gently,"It's ok. I don't even remember how they looked. They were murdered by werewolves. I was just 4 at that time. My grandfather Zaar the first Valac king, saved me and was killed. My uncle and aunt were also killed protecting their newborn son Zephyr along with one of our witches. Felicia, our lead witch protected him and hid him all these centuries. Since he was a pure-blood and the next king, they kept him in secret. Nobody bothered to even look at me even though I was the eldest prince and rightful king but not a pureblood. And when I got of age, it turn worse. I had no abilities so the King Markus, my youngest uncle banished me. Now, his son Vincent, the youngest of my cousins is the King whereas Zephyr was still in hiding until now...I hate those Valacs hence I'm not interested in going there even though now I h...." He stopped saying.

"Huh...?"

"Nothing..." he replied. He was about to say something but he didn't continued. It must be something he don't want me to know.

"What is that ?" I asked pointing towards the sickle- shaped monument in white marble. I always saw it through my balcony but never asked anyone.

"Oh you don't know that? It the symbol of House Gregor - a crescent moon. House Reese also has the same. The Valacs and Bloodstones have half-moons. The only difference between them all is the direction they face. Each direction has a unique kind of ability associated with it".

"Only the royal family vampires have these abilities?" I further questioned with curiosity.

"Every royal has these abilities. I am the only exception. But a few vampires who don't have moonstones but still have abilities are also out there. They get it through sheer luck like Rowan who had sight, to sense a person's mana,its nature and past. But those abilities are not so powerful like royals. And then again, there are families who live completely on animal blood and never tasted any human blood.

A few of them or all may or may not have abilities. Though their physical strength is incomparable to us, almost like an average vampire but their abilities are more powerful than us. They are called Ions. The Drakens of the councill are the only ions I know in so many centuries because for vampires its almost next to impossible to control their thirst for human blood" he replied explaining.

My blood ran cold at the mention of Rowan and Scott. I couldn't hear a word what he was saying and only those incidents flashed before my eyes. Tears welled up my eyes and I was about to collapse but instead I was seized into a tight embrace and I let myself drown in that warmth...

Chapter 19 – Feel

No...Stop

Please don't do this...

No...

I opened my eyes panting heavily. And as everyday Claude was with me holding my hand. My hand was wet due to sweat. My forehead and hair were drenched in a cold sweat. My body was shivering with fear and my heart was racing in my chest screaming for air. Claude quickly gave me the potion which Eva made especially for my nightmares but it seemed to have no effect.

Its been almost a month since that incident. I was somehow recovering from my trauma with Claude next to me. He stayed all those nights when I was struggling to sleep.

It was the same when Jeremy assaulted me and those dreadful dreams kept haunting me but the episodes were less frequent up until now. That was a bad phase of my life and I took almost two years to recover from that trauma that too not completely. And the current chain of events made it worse.

I had to go through it all alone in my past but not this time. I have Claude with me. He never left me alone as he said. Though I am getting those dreadful dreams it's getting better every day. This was the first nightmare in the last two weeks. I'm getting better and feeling happy and Claude was the reason behind it.

Things have got so good between us. All these days nobody bothered me. Neither Cecily nor William or others. I used to play video games with Charles and Claude though I didn't enjoy them much. Claude use not take me to the mountain top to see the sunrise and constellations. But more than the view, I loved his company.

I love to be with him.

I love his cooking.

I love his habit of always tunneling his fingers through his hair.

I love his awful singing or to be precise screaming songs with incorrect lyrics and when he doesn't know what next line is he just hum some tune...

I love it when he always pokes my forehead and smiles at me.

I love it when he wrap me in his arms

I love it when he gently smiles at me

I love it when he stares me every single night until I sleep

I love it when he calls my name.

I love everything about him...

"Serena...It's ok. I am here"

I love it every time when I get scared and he assures me I am here...for you...

What is this feeling...Is it love...I asked myself but I didn't get any answers.

I threw my legs across the bed and drank some water. Claude stood in front of me. I could see his bare muscles from his sleeveless black t-shirt. The sun rays beamed on his tanned skin-enhancing his features.

"Don't bath. Today we're going to a lake. Its summer solstice today", he sounded excited.

I didn't know swimming but I still agreed. The sun was burning up and the sky was bright. I brushed and got fresh. I quickly went through my closet and picked up an aqua blue bikini and a white tank top with black capris and left downstairs.

Everyone was present in there summer clothes shorts, sarongs, tank tops, crop tops. Some of the boys only had their shorts on. Claude stood there with a smile on his face. The witches were busy. It seemed they weren't going to come. As soon as I came, William said, "I think all are here now. Cassandra, we would be back by afternoon. Please look over Charles. Has anyone got a beach ball?"

"I have got it" someone replied.

"Very well. Let's go" and the next second everyone vanished including William. I had never seen him smile or excited about anything. He must really love the lake. It was only me and Claude and the witches.

"I'll carry you. Hold on tight ok" he gripped my waist in his arm pressing me towards his chest.

"Don't leave me mid-air this time" I warned him but it came out more as a request than a warning.

"Yes mam..." he lifted me and I grabbed him tightly with my legs around his waist and said, "I'm ready when you are".

"I'm ready" and the next second we were in the air jumping from one tree to another. I tightened my grip on him and closed my eyes. Even though it was I did this many times but I still felt scared. I felt very protective in his arms.

After about twenty minutes we landed down. There were a lot of vampires than those in the castle. I could see a lot of new faces along with Ivan.

"I didn't know you were here," he mumbled at Ivan.

"Hello, gorgeous...How are you" Ivan greeted me completely ignoring Claude. A girl followed him. She was practically hissing at me. She was incredibly beautiful and had green eyes and long blonde locks and crimson red lipstick. She wore a purple bikini that exposed her flawless curves. A crescent moon was etched near her navel.

I saw Ivan he was topless and wore black trunks. He too had the same crescent moon on his chest.

"I'm fine...Thank you" I replied politely smiling at him.

"Wanna swim with me" he winked at me and I heard a hiss from the green-eyed girl. Must be his girlfriend.

Before I could reply Claude said, "No, she will be with me" looping his hand on my waist and by this time I could see the green-eyes turning red blood red...Now, what's her issue...

By this time Claude and I were already away from Ivan's group. I gazed around and all vampires were getting changed in bikinis and shorts and trunks. The temperature was rising due to the hotness of this place more than the sun...

Ivan left with a few women and the girl left with him but was still throwing daggers at me from behind the tree.

"Claude, who..." I turned to ask Claude who was the girl but I was speechless as I saw him in nothing but grey shorts. I kept gaping at him as he came closer "Aren't you going to change?"

"Uh...No...I'm fine." I gazed down at the ground in embarrassment. I couldn't swim but still, I had a bikini. I thought it would only be me and Claude. But seeing these many people, not to mention those seductive females surrounding him, I got very self-conscious. All women had perfect bodies with big bust and hips and not to mention smoking-hot revealing bikinis. I looked around myself and at this point in time, I was the only one who was fully covered.

"You're so cute..." he smiled at me and pulled me closer, "Its ok. You can just sit at the deck and enjoy the view. "

I sat at one of the chairs. The woman right next to me was almost naked with nothing but strings as her bikini. Many other females had similarly styled bikinis on them with bold lipsticks and blossomed chests. Claude went to play volleyball with William who was enjoying and literally laughing. Some of the vampires were swimming, some were making out without a care who is watching. Some were practically running on the water with their supersonic speed. A few of them were having a sunbath. I wonder if vampires even get a tan. My eyes wandered towards Rose and Jared. They were sitting far aside from the crowd, hand-in-hand and gazing at the lake. They really made a cute couple.

"Hey..."

"Hi...", it was Levi in red trunks. His body screamed macho. He had a well-built body just like others.

" May I sit here?" he asked me pointing towards the seat to my left. I simply nodded.

"Didn't go for a swim?" he asked.

"I can't swim...You didn't go?" I asked.

"I don't feel like..." though he was sitting next to me, his gaze was directed towards Rose and Jared. Come to think of it, whenever I see them, all the three are always together except when the couple is having a moment.

"They look good together," I said following his sight to which he just gave a light smile. It was as if he's forcing the smile with a strained look. Does he not like his friends being happy...Or does he also like Rose...

I glanced at my back but Claude was not there. Neither was William. I panicked and my eyes searching him.

"Claude has gone with William and few vampires towards the Black Mountain. They'll be back in a few minutes. He's asked me to look after you"

"Why"

"It's kind of a tradition set by William. Whenever we come to Lake, we have a race till Black Mountain. The winning team gets to have a wish fulfilled from Cassandra" he replied but his eyes were still fixed at the couple.

"Oh... You didn't participate?"

"Even though I win she can't fulfill my wish" his face was sad and his voice quavering. I was about to ask him but a scream let out my mouth. It was all red thick metallic blood all over my stomach.

"What is this?", I screamed. I felt gross with all that sickening rotten smell.

" Irene..." Levi raised his voice in anger at a girl. The same green-eyed girl who was throwing daggers at me earlier. She twirled her fingers through the locks of hair and said, "It's bear's blood. It didn't suit my taste, smelled awful, and was about to throw it but oops my hand slipped" she gave an evil smirk and left.

The putrid odor was so sharp I was almost choking for air. I ran towards the nearby tree and threw up.

"You need to wash up," he said and took me near the lakeshore. The other vampires made way for us and cleared that side of the lake. It seems they were scared of Levi.

"Who's she and what's her problem?" I started rinsing the blood with water.

"Irene. Ivan's sister. She's just jealous. Ignore her"

"But why me. I never met her"

"She doesn't like Claude spending time with you. She loves Claude..."

His words hurt my heart like a knife stabbing me again and again.

"And Claude?" I asked my voice wavering hoping to get an answer which I want to hear.

"I don't know..." he replied with a plain face and continued, "I think the smell won't go. I'll go get a t-shirt for you to change".

Luckily, there were very few people around me. I quickly removed my white tank top and now I was there with only my blue bikini and black Capri. I started rubbing it on the stone with water.

I felt a few of them staring at me. They might be thinking I'm a nutcase. I just wanted to Levi return back as fast as possible.

****

Claude's POV

Reaching the peak I saw William's team had already mounted their flag. I was totally distracted and so I lost. I just hope Serena is ok. Though it was just a matter of a few minutes still I'm worried. I had to ask Levi to look after her until I'm back.

"You're not in the form today", William patted my back

" Ya... Can we leave now? " I just wanted to go back asap. But he was in his own happy bubble. He really enjoyed it I can see...

"Sure...Guys let's go back..." And we left.

As soon as I reached I saw Levi near the bushes and I quickly followed. He was shuffling something in his backpack.

"What are you doing here? Where's Serena?"

By now, all the contents of his bag were on display - his earphones, a nunchuck, tissues, blood pouch, a pair of shorts, Rose's photo along with a used coffee mug with a lipstick mark. Wtf...

"She's at the lakeshore. Irene threw bear blood on her so I was finding her a change of clothes but my t-shirt is not here".

"Irene" this girl is going to be the end of my patience. "Here's mine. Let's go" I followed him to the shore. I saw a lot of males gazing in a particular direction. I peeked to check out and it was her...my love...

She was sitting near the stones rubbing her shirt with water totally oblivious of the males leering at her. She looked breathtakingly beautiful in her bikini. Innocent and graceful unlike those slutty vampires. Her milky skin radiated under the sunlight. It looked so lustrous and smooth that I couldn't stop staring. Her brunette locks flowed one side all the way from her neck with their tips submerged in water. My senses were clouded with desire but soon turned into anger when I saw the other vampires ogling her with lustful eyes. I let out a small snarl with my fangs out to let them know I'm here and the girl they are gawking is mine. Within a few seconds, they cleared my path and I continued walking towards her.

Levi followed me and I was happy he was unfazed by the sight. He had his eyes only for Rose. As we approached I asked him to leave. She turned behind me and was very flustered looking at me. She consciously covered her chest with her delicate arms. Her cheeks were blushing red. I handed her my t-shirt and she quickly wore it. She looked so cute in it. It was hanging from one of her shoulders and looked like a dress covering her thighs. I gave her my hand and pulled her up on her feet.

"Let's go...you must be hungry," I said.

We sat on a deck chair and Levi bought the straw basket which I prepared for her.

"What's in this", she asked.

" Some food. We would leave by evening so I thought to pack some for you".

"Thanks" she blushed as I handed a sandwich. I packed enough for both of us though I enjoyed watching her eat. I grabbed an apple and gave her company while Levi cleared everyone slowly from around us.

"So she's your fiancee?" I was distracted by her sudden question.

"Huh..."

"Irene..." she whispered.

"No, she's not. She's just obsessed with me. I don't love her", I expressed my disgust.

I love you

I wanted to scream and tell her my feelings but I don't want to rush and want her to feel, the reason I threatened everyone not to disclose my secret my feelings my love to her...I want to be the one to tell her...

Chapter 20 - Mysterious

Serena's POV

"She was human?" I was surprised at the fact I just learned about Rose.

"Yes. Levi used to stalk her when she was a human and then one day she met in an accident and was about to die so Levi saved her and bought her here" Claude replied sipping his blood-wine while I was munching cookies. That explains the way he always stares at her so lovingly.

"Unfortunately, Jared asked her before and they are happy ever since" he continued.

Poor Levi

"How does one become a vampire?" I was very curious to know how does it happen. Though I was not sure if Claude would disclose it. It might be a secret but still, I asked.

He let out a sigh, "Royals and Ions can turn humans into vampires on a new moon by making the latter drink their blood. Though only males have this skill since females can give birth. But nobody does it nowadays"

"Why?"

"Because some of their powers get transported to the turned vampires. So the royals don't do that anymore. There are a very few vampires who are turned..."

"So Rose also has powers?" I wiped my face of the crumbs.

"Nope. William turned her after we lost moonstones" he answered gazing in his goblet. I wonder if Claude had turn anyone...

"Have you ever turned anyone?" I asked and he was caught off guard by my question. He lifted his eyes which met mine. They were flickering between the shades of brown and golden.

"No. My mother was a human so I can't" he let out a sad sigh "I wish I could...Nevermind...I wanted to know you have a dress? As in a party dress?" I was completely astonished by his question.

I didn't have any. All I had were a few old frocks that belonged to Cecily and some ragged old clothes which I wore along with Claude's t-shirts as a nightdress, "No, I don't. What happen?"

"There's a grand party in two days from now. Do you know Michael Dean?" he asked.

My eyes widened at the name. The CEO of my workplace along with the owner of the leading food industry, previously a model and now a successful entrepreneur and a billionaire.

"Well, he is a vampire...William turned him a few years ago. He struck a deal with Will that in exchange for money and manpower he wants immortality. So basically our contractual humans and any legal issues are all handled by him. But he still likes his human life and he prefers to stay among them and he's totally into money. Every year he throws a party. So the royals, the ions, and businessmen I mean humans are all invited. Though the ions don't go there and the Valacs despise him because of the fact that he loves to be with humans. So I think only Gregors and Reese families would be there and you'll come with us..." he stated.

I just couldn't believe the most popular person on BT would be a vampire. But I was glad I am finally going somewhere out of this forest for a change.

***

"Rose and Jared are going to go to the nearest town to get her a dress. So get ready in an hour. We'll also go" Claude said tunneling his fingers through his hair. I just love it when he does this...

I threw my legs out of the bed and left for a quick shower. I yanked a light purple chiffon dress that perfectly fitted my curves. I matched it with a golden bracelet with a crescent moon which Claude bought for me and left downstairs.

"Hey..."

"Hi Rose" I replied. She was plunged to Jared as usual. Levi and the witches too were present.

"Ready...Are we?" Claude asked.

"I had already picked a dress so I won't be coming," Eva said.

"I'll come. I need a few adjustments in mine" Cassandra said fuming in anger. It seems the designer is going to have a hard time today.

Two black audis stood in front of the gate. Everyone took the first one whereas Claude dragged me to the second one. He pulled the door for me and as soon as I sat he went to the driver's seat.

"Is it far?" I asked. I was not so good with cars. Motion sickness.....

"No just one hour drive. Levi and others would reach first. I'd ask him to scout the area before we reach" he replied.

One hour is too much. But considering the fact, that we stay so deep inside the forest it'll take an hour or more to reach. Opening the window, I let the fresh air come in.

"Levi is a very good person. Initially, he seemed very reserved but slowly he opened up" I started the conversation. A small smile visible on his face, "Yes. He's the only male I can trust you with, in this house not even William".

Wait what... Isn't William close to him...

"Why so?"

"Because he's my childhood friend. He was the only person who looked after me while I was with the Valacs and joined me when I was banished. His parents were warriors. They taught the royal kids how to fight. They were specifically told not to teach me. However, Levi used to learn himself and teach me all that. Those days were so good. Since most vampires were active at night, we use to sneak out of the castle early morning and go far away from the forest to the city, a human garden to learn. He's the best fighter after me. I think, no I'm sure, not even William or Ivan would stand a chance in hand-to-hand combat with him" he proudly stated as if he's talking about his own child.

"Pretty strong" I exclaimed.

"Not as much to beat me" he smirked.

"So he is your best friend I suppose" I know I was getting personal but I just wanted to know him more.

"Yes...You can say that" he smiled.

And what about me? I asked him in my mind but didn't have the courage to say it. What am I to him? He always stays to close to me, never let me get out of his sight. But why is he doing that? Does he feel the same what I am feeling for him...

The car stopped and we got down. The street was pretty lively for a town. Small kids were playing catch in the playground. Men and women were chatting in groups. One side of the road was lined with boutiques and showrooms. The other side had small rowhouses. We walked and reached a boutique named 'Sew In Style'. It was a cute little store from outside. As we walked in, I realized it was ten times bigger than it seemed from outside. A thin man in a floral shirt and pink dyed hair came and greeted us.

"Welcome...", he came forward and air-kissed Levi and Jared. Both of them had enraged looks while I was surprised and I looked at Claude who seems unfazed. Rose chuckled at them.

"Bobby you bastard" Jared was about to punch him but Rose calmed him.

"The next time you do that I'll kill you", Levi fumed in anger.

"I don't mind to die in your strong hands" Bobby replied flicking his pink hairs with a pout.

"F*ck Off" he swore verbal profanities at Bobby who seemed unaffected.

"You first come with me. What did you do to my dress? I asked you specifically to keep it decent" Cassandra screamed at him.

"You need to show some cleavage dear" Bobby replied following a weird gesture towards his chest.

"I don't want to...Fix it now" Cassandra raged. By this time Bobby was victim to almost everyone's wrath.

"Ok...ok...Julia sweety please help our guests. I need to work on Cassie's dress" he left along with Cassandra in the VIP room.

"Its Cassandra for you" was all I could hear before she stormed out. A blonde girl came out in her formal dress.

"How can I help you, Madam?" she asked.

" Party gowns for us and a suit for him" Rose pointed towards Levi. A man appeared and took Levi to the men's section and the rest of us followed the female attendant towards another room. It was big with racks of dresses everywhere. The golden lights reflected the marble flooring and shined on those dresses. A few mannequins stood on my left with gowns and short dresses each of them looked a masterpiece. There were a few changing rooms ahead to the right side while few couches were kept in the center. We took the couches and the attendants came with a lot of dresses. All of them were beautiful. Rose selected three of them and a few for me as well.

"Let's go" she dragged me towards the changing rooms while the boys kept looking at us. She picked a silver shimmering dress and I picked a plain pink mermaid skirt long gown. The gown had a side chain and I easily slipped in it but I wasn't able to zip the chain. I think the dress was small for me. I quickly got changed into another three dresses. All were good but either uncomfortable or not my size. I selected another dress while Rose came out mumbling something.

"Why aren't you dressed?" she asked me not seeing me in the pink dress.

"It was not my size. It was too small".

"Ohh...there are too many. Take your time and select. I didn't like this dress. It's too uncomfortable. Too much glittery" she said while leaving the dress on the rack and scanning the other racks picking up an aquamarine fish cut dress. It was indeed beautiful. She went towards the changing room.

I checked all the racks and a red strapless dress caught my eyes. I picked it up and went to the changing room next to her. I held the dress on my chest. I knew it would look good on me so I stripped and got changed into it. I struggled to zip it since it was at the back but somehow managed. The dress looked ravishing and bold. I felt I'm seeing an evil version of myself in the mirror. My bust looked vulnerable and exposed and the dress had a long slit on the left leg. Though it looks sexy but too much skin. Wrong choice...I can't wear something like this. I started to get change. But the zip was jammed. It didn't come off. I struggled harder but was left with a strain in my shoulders.

"Rose...Could you please help me unzip this?"

"Rose..."

"Are you there?"

I heard no reply. I saw the door of the cubicle in the mirror opening behind me and Claude walked in "She left to..." and he stopped. He kept staring at me.

" I...I just wanted her help to unzip this" I said slowly. He closed the door behind. The cubicle was too small to fit in both of us. He stood too close and my heart started beating fast against my chest. I couldn't bring myself to turn around and look at him so I kept staring at him through the mirror. I was too embarrassed to be so close to him in this cramped place.

"You look gorgeous, he said as he stepped in.

"Thanks. But I don't plan to..." he moved towards me and placed his hands on my waist and his neck rested at my shoulder. My breath was caught in my throat. I kept looking at the mirror and so did he. My breathing was uneven and I was restless "to wear this" I finished my sentence.

"Why? You look beautiful..." his lips grazed my bare skin near my shoulder and a moan of pleasure was about to leave my mouth but I controlled myself.

"It's too revealing," I said slowly. His eyes drifted from my eyes to my chest in the mirror. I felt nervous and my breathing paced up.

"It is indeed", he replied while his eyes turned pitch black. Now I was scared...

His grip on my waist got tighter and he pulled me towards him. My back touched his hard chest and our eyes were met each other in the mirror. His face lowered near my neck still facing the mirror, his temple touched mine and I could feel one of his arms gliding near my zip. My heart was thumping in my chest loudly and I could see my breasts rising and falling due to the way I was breathing. His lips brushed my temples and my ears and soon the zip came off. I could feel his breath over my shoulders while his eyes still were black.

"It's done. I'll just go..." and he took off while I held the dress tightly at my chest and shut the door. I felt so tired I just sat down with my back at the door. What was that just now? What was he trying to do? Those pitch-black eyes were scary as well as captivating...I quickly got changed in my dress and went out.

"Sweety...What are you doing? Leave that dress. I've already one dress in my mind. You would look stunning in it" Bobby dragged me towards another room and handed me a gorgeous dress and I knew it was the one for me.

It was a long golden mermaid high neck dress beaded with sequins and intricate golden patchwork. It was studded with stones around the neck which continued as a strap through my shoulders in a v shape showing a little cleavage. The dress fitted my curves perfectly till thigh and flowed down.

"Here are golden heels and a golden bangle. You look like a golden deity" and he air-kissed me.

"Thanks" I quickly got changed and asked him to pack the dress.

We took all the dresses and sat in the car. Claude, Rose, and Jared were left behind whereas the others already left for the castle.

"Claude, we would get down here and come after some time. You guys can go ahead" Jared said.

"Where you're going?" he asked.

"There's a flower exhibition today and Rose wants to see. So we'll just have a look" he replied smiling at Rose.

Flower exhibition. Sounds interesting. I also wanna go. Sensing my change of expressions he asked me, "You wanna go?"

"Yes..."

"Let's all go then..." he announced and followed Jared's direction.

We took a left and reached a big lawn. We collected our passes and went in. There were many beautiful flowers. Different colors of roses and lilies I never knew existed stood on one side whereas jasmine, marigolds, petunia, phlox, anemones, and many others were scattered all over. Their overlapping sweet scents and the colorful sight left me mesmerized. The pond was filled with water lilies and lotuses. The place was flooded with people. It reminded me of the subway in the evening hours. Soon Claude squeezed my hand and I stopped, "There is someone here I know. Can you stay with Jared and Rose? I'll be back in five minutes. Don't go wandering alone"

"Ok..."

He left somewhere in the crowd. I turned back to see Rose but they were not there. I moved fast but couldn't see anyone. There was a huge crowd near the tulips. I wanted to see tulips but I dropped the idea, seeing the flock of people. I tried to search but couldn't find them. Walking I came towards a small corner of the garden where nobody was there. It was filled with white hellebores and smelled pleasant. I wonder why nobody is coming here. The flowers are so beautiful and delicate. I tried to touch one of those and I felt a cold hand on my shoulder.

"Didn't you see the skull sign outside this area?" a man in a blue hood with black sunglasses asked me.

"No... "

"It' nelium oleander. It's poisonous. You would be dead if you inhale any of its pores" he said and I quickly backed off "Sorry, I didn't know. Thanks...". I was such a fool I mentally slapped myself.

"Lucky, I was here. So wh..." he was about to ask something but he looked around and took off so fast I couldn't see him anymore almost like a vampire.

"Serena...Here you are. Didn't you see the danger sign? I was losing my mind searching for you. We need to leave. I can sense a few other vampires" Claude hugged me and dragged me out of that garden.

That person...His speed and his cold touch...Was he a vampire...Who was he and...why did he run away...

Chapter 21 - Depth

Serena's POV

My skin looked sun-lit dazzling. I specifically asked Anna to keep it simple. She kept my lipstick nude along with a little golden shimmer on my lids that perfectly matched with my golden attire. My hair was kept into a loose messy fishtail braid. I didn't wear the golden bangle which came with the dress instead kept the golden bracelet which Claude gave me. Putting my golden stilettos I left downstairs.

William stood alone sipping blood-wine in his black tuxedo and gel-set hair. He looked handsome. He glanced at me, "You took a long time to get ready. Claude and Levi had gone ahead. They have some urgent business to attend. They'll meet us directly at the party. Everyone else had left. So you'll go with me and Charles".

Oh no. Though William didn't bother me from a few weeks which was a bit weird I was still scared of him. He has this scary aura around him and that short-temper is too intimidating. At least Charles is there with us.

" Serena...You look like a fairy" Charles ran towards me and kissed my cheek. William widened his eyes towards the little boy in anger.

"You look like a charming little prince" I smile at him and pecked his forehead and we left. I took the passenger seat whereas William drove the car. Charles sat behind playing some game on his phone.

The journey was so suffocating. Neither of us said anything and we drove silently. It was almost sunset. I just wanted to reach asap. The silence was slowly killing me until he broke it, "You look beautiful".

I was dumbfounded at his words. Is this William sitting next to me? Is he possessed? I mentally pinched myself. I couldn't believe my ears, " Umm...Thanks" I responded. And then again the silence continued but I was comparatively relaxed now. The smell of petrol and air was mixed in our perfumes and the movement of the car was increasing my motion sickness. I just want to get out of this car.

"Are you feeling ok?" he appeared worried when I bend myself with my palm on my mouth.

"Motion sickness..." I said somehow controlling my urge to puke. He quickly opened the window on my side and I took a deep long breath. It felt like I've been released from a choke. It felt so better.

It was a long journey. It took us almost two hours to reach our destination. His mansion was as big as William's but had more of a modern touch whereas William's was a gothic style. The mansion was more like a big fancy fortress on a hilltop on the outskirts of the forest, covered with tall fencing. A river was flowing adjacent to the hill. A small statue of a letter 'D' with its mirror image stood outside near the fountain. It was the trademark of Dean Foods, also the one I had on my uniform.

William grabbed the door for me and I got out along with Charles. Both Charles and William look exactly the same in similar black tux and gel-set hair that too in a similar style. It was kinda cute. As soon as we entered the main building, several people stood there drinking and talking. I scanned my eyes for Claude but didn't see him. A few people were gazing at us as we made our entrance.

Suddenly, out of nowhere a girl in black cross neck dress appeared. I saw her carefully it was Ashley Ryle, the supermodel who was always featured in 'The Glam'. She had silky short blonde hair and hazel eyes with a skinny figure. Out of nowhere, she hugged William, "Will...baby... Where were you and who's this girl with you?"

She seemed tipsy and reeked of alcohol. Maybe she's William's girlfriend. "How much did you drink Ash?" He nicknames her and expresses his concern. She's definitely his girlfriend. Jared and Rose came towards us. Jared wore a navy blue suit whereas Rose had the same aquamarine dress which she selected that day. Cassandra had a dark green gown and Eva had a sky blue gown. All of them look wonderful.

"Serena you look stunning. All eyes are on you today..." I blushed and thanked them while William left with Ashley.

"Where's Claude?" I asked Jared.

"I didn't see him yet. Neither Levi. Don't worry just enjoy the party. He'll be here soon" he smiled at me and took off with Rose at the dancefloor.

I looked back but Cassandra had left to talk to some people in white suits taking Charles along. I was left with Eva.

"Let's eat something... I'm hungry" she dragged us towards the food section. She ate a few cheesecakes and chicken balls. I was in no mood to eat. My stomach was still upset due to the long ride we had "I think I'll just find something to drink. My stomach doesn't feel good".

I took off near the bar. A cute boy who seemed younger than me stood at the counter. I was in a dilemma whether I should go there or not but I went.

"Hello, what would you like to miss?" he smiled.

"Uh...Do you perhaps have lemonade or lemon juice?" I asked feeling embarrassed asking for such a thing at this big party, even though I was an adult. But I had never ever tasted liquor and right now only lemon juice was going to calm my stomach.

He chuckled slightly raising his brow, "I'm afraid we don't have that. We only have alcoholic drinks here. Should I get you wine. It would have less alcohol in it?" he thoughtfully asked.

"No that's ok" I smiled at him.

"Hey, sexy. I'll get you a drink" a drunk man appeared out of nowhere and held my wrist and pushed his glass towards me.

"No thanks. I'm done. I'll leave...my friends are waiting" I replied politely and tried to free myself from his grasp.

"That big guy...Your boyfriend is busy with the blonde babe. Just come with me. I'll show you a great time" he said with an evil smirk pulling me towards him. The bartender looked angry and interfered, "Sir, Please let her go".

"You filthy creature. How dare you. Don't you know who I am?" the man shouted on the bartender earning some audience before he was stopped by another person. A man in jet black hair, light brown eyes, and white tux came out of nowhere and grasped the man's hand, "Let the lady go now..." he calmly stated and the man left my wrist and went away without a single word. It was hypnosis. I noticed the bar-tender was glad but still it felt like he's pissed on the black hair man who just helped me.

"Thanks" I thanked the black-haired man.

He chuckled, "You sure do attract a lot of trouble".

" Sorry?" I was confused at his words but he kept glaring at me.

"Nothing...I'm Luke. What's your name?" he asked.

"Serena" my voice came out very slow. My stomach was still not good. The urge to puke was increasing by every moment and my palm was drenched in cold sweat.

He handed me a can of lemon soda out of nowhere and I was speechless. Was he stalking me? Should I even accept this drink? It might be spiked or worst case drugged. I kept staring at the bottle and he chuckled, "Don't worry its not drugged. Its still sealed. I got it from the nearby vending machine".

"How did you know?" I was surprised seeing the lemonade though it was canned but still enough so quench my thirst.

"I heard you" he gave a smug smile but I was still delighted to have it. I quickly gulped it down my throat.

"Thanks"

"What a beautiful lady like you doing here alone?" he asked making me blush.

"I was with a few people...friends... but everyone left somewhere and I don't know anyone here" I replied my eyes still searching Claude.

"Well, you know me now" he showed his shiny pearls and continued, "No alcohol?"

"Never ever had..." and I lowered my head in embarrassment. I could feel a lot of people staring at us or at him to be precise. He was indeed good-looking with those black hair and toned body. He must be a famous personality or a model.

"You must be very popular. People are staring you" I stated.

"It's you who they are looking at not me. You're exceptionally gorgeous" I blushed at the comment when Charles came running towards me and tugged my hand.

"Let's go. Cassie wants you to come with us" and he dragged me towards the first floor. I waived a bye at Luke and left.

Unknown POV

I came here just for fun to spend some time among humans. Though I also wanted to scoop some information on the two vampire kings but the main reason was only to kill some time. Then a scent hit me, honey, vanilla with strawberries and waterfall. I know waterfall is no smell but it felt so fresh.

I knew she was here. The last time I saw her she was about to touch those nasty flowers with her delicate hands. She was the most beautiful woman I ever seen all these centuries but was a human. I wanted to talk to her without revealing myself but strong mana distracted me that day and I had to leave. But now she's here again. This time I'm not letting her go.

She was standing at the bar asking for a lemonade. So cute...I chuckled at her innocence but she seemed very restless as if she's about to throw up. I'm not letting this golden chance go. I ran towards the vending machine near parking lot and got a lemonade.

When I returned, my sight turned red blood red seeing a disgusting trash of a man who held her wrist and she was struggling to get off. Her eyes were welled up with unshed tears and fear was visible in her eyes. She looked stunning in her golden glory like a goddess. Unlike those skinny, busty vampires I met, she was decent but sexy, innocent, and irresistible. I quickly went towards her and made the vile man look into my eyes "Let the lady go now...". and compelled him to go. Had this not been a human party, I would have torn him to shreds.

She smiled at me with those pink soft lips and thanked me. She didn't recognize me from the flower exhibition. Luckily, I disguised myself today as well. The young wolf at the counter recognized me and growled at me but couldn't do anything since there were humans. Though he was pathetic weak little dog.

She talked to me. Her voice was sweet angelic. Apparently, she was here with some friends. I could sense a lot of males both vampires and humans staring at her in lustful eyes. The desire was clearly seen in those hungry eyes whereas some women also gazed her in jealousy. Serena was her name which suited her tranquility and calm aura. It just made me wanna ravish her.

I talked to her for some time but suddenly I felt small mana, a brat came running towards her and dragged her away from me. But the fact that shocked me was he was a vampire...

She is human. How does she know that vampire brat? Does she know our existence or is she mated to one of those vampires, the thought itself boiled my blood? I couldn't see a mark on her and she smelled virgin. Mate or not I'll have her for myself and that is for sure. I just want to know who exactly she is.

I followed her and she was sitting with a group of people along with the brat. All of them had immensely powerful manas a few of them were witches and the rest vampires and all males. She was the only human in the bunch. Those dimwits didn't even notice my presence or my mana. I doubt they can even make out I'm a vampire or a human simply looking at me. I had masked my mana so well and my ability disguises me as a human. No vampire had ever caught me being one of them. But it doesn't work on the wolves.

I overheard their conversation. The two strongest manas belonged to the crescent moon Kings along with their witches and a few more vampires sat there along with Michael and his women. But what do they want with Serena? I need to find out...

Serena's POV

Charles made me sit next to him. William was there without Ashley and Ivan sat next to a lady who seemed gorgeous but in the late thirties. Claude was still nowhere.

"Hello Serena" Ivan greeted me. He was a bit more formal today. I greeted him back.

"So it's her?" the lady stared at me in disgust and flicked her blonde hairs. Irene sat next to her in a pink cocktail dress. She looked cute and the woman somewhat resembled her or to be correct she resembled the woman. I think I know who she was…Ivan's mother.

"Yes," Irene spatted in hatred.

"Let's leave dear. This filth is not worth our time" the queen arrogantly humiliated me and left with her daughter. Ivan followed them in anger.

"Ignore her" Eva smiled at me and I took a seat next to her. Everyone else seem to enjoy their blood-wine which was served only on this floor.

The evening went well. I enjoyed the variety of food and met a few popular figures who I only saw on TV. Though I was not sure which one of them were vampires and which were humans. Everyone was good to me. Everything was perfect except Claude. I really wanted to be with him dance with him.

Suddenly my throat started itching. I was allergic to tuna but I remembered it was not on the menu. It must be one of those fishes. I quickly grabbed a glass of water but the throat still felt sore and was woresining by every second.

"Excuse me...Where's the restroom" I asked a waiter coughing all my way.

"The one on this floor is under maintainenece. The nearest one is straight at the end of that hallway on the second floor " he pointed upwards. Everone was busy talking with the witches from Reese.

"Charles, could you go and wait with William or Cassie. I need to use the restroom. I'll be back in few minutes" I said him he was busy in his game and he replied "Yep".

I rushed towards the staircase and already had feeling to puke. I threw up and I was scared to death seeing only blood in the basin. I tried to scream but I couldn't utter a single word or cry. I couldn't even wimper. I lost my voice.

I checked myself in the mirror and slowly my arms and neck started to fade. I screamed in panic but a pin drop silence was all there in the restroom. Slowly my whole body vanished into thin air. I could feel my surrounding but wasn't able to talk or see my body. I felt my body being lifted and within a second I was on the terrace.

Cold air stinged me. My whole body felt numb but slowly appearing again I could see my arms and other parts. It was as if I'm in some sort of nightmare.

"How dare you upset our princess. You had your eyes on her love as well as her brother. You are nothing but a wh*re. You deserve to die" I heard a familiar coarse voice but couldn't see anyone.

'Who is here? Who is this?' I screamed but I couldn't hear myself. My voice was still subdued.

"Your Death" and I was being lifted in air and held onto the railing. I could see the river gushing below. I screamed and screamed but nothing was heard. I cried my heart out and begged for mercy but then I felt myself in mid-air with slowly consumed by the depths of the water.

Chapter 22 - Motives

Claude's POV

" Once they knew about the prophecy and the ritual, they killed the old witch and attained her powers. The Bloodstones were manipulated into wiping the Reese and Gregors. Kairo was an idiot, just a pawn. He didn't saw through their real plan. Vengeance was never their motive. They were after the moodstones" the little curly cat-eyed witch stated. Never for a moment, she got down from her wolf. The whole time the wolf kept his eyes on us monitoring our every movement. I could feel his anxious heartbeat in this silent forest very prominently along with soft growls. Both their manas were as powerful as Levi. I still don't understand why she specifically asked William to send me here. I wanted to be with Serena but since this concerns her, its better I came.

" My only concern is why Serena? She's not even a vampire? " the wolf turned into a muscular naked man as Crystal got down from him and appeared calm. She gave a shawl from her bag which he wrapped around his waist. I gestured Levi to ease up. The mana the both were emitting was very warm and friendly.

The wolf man held his mate closer to him possesively and snaked his arm around her waist as a warning for us to stay away from her. She seemed embarrassed as she spoke up, "According to the prophecy, Serena's the one born on a mystical day and time, when all the con-stellations formed a celestial pattern we call 'Solomon's seal' - a star inside a circle, like the one which we witches use for enchantments. Its an extremely rare phenomenon and the first to occur in thousands and millions of years. It lasted only for a few seconds, those exact seconds when she was born, the only living person born at that moment, in the whole world. And as per my prediction, the same astronomical shape won't be formed again for another million years. "

"What are their intentions?"

" I don't know yet. But I can help you with one thing for which I called you. William said you love her a lot and so only it had to be you that could do this" she removed a blue gem from her bag and moved towards me.

"What's that?" I asked gazing the blue gem.

"Its a guard stone I got from the tomb of Aradia. It's a gem that promotes spiritual awakening, serenity, and tranquility. If it glows red on your touch, you are the guardian and if you are not, it'll burn your hand" the wolf man smirked at me as Crystal finished her explanation.

While I hoped I'm her guardian so that I can be with her all the time and sense her in danger. The aqua blue gem looked very shiny. She held it delicately and handed it to me. The wolf man followed her protectively stood next to her. I took the gem in my hand. But to my surprise, it didn't glow red, neither it burnt me. Both of them kept looking at me in shock.

"It didn't burn neither it glowed. What does that mean?" I questioned. Is this woman making a fool out of me?

"It means you love her. You don't mean her any harm. The stone is living. It understood your feelings and won't hurt you like how it didnt hurt me. But unfortunately, you are not the guardian" she stated casually while the wolfman let a sigh of relief. May be now he's convinced I am not after his mate.

Levi interrupted, "But it doesn't mean we can rub it on everyone's arm to check and burn them". In a way he was correct but I don't mind burning anyone for my Serena. A chuckle went down through her lips, "As I said the stone is living and as soon as it recognizes the guardians are near it'll glow in its blue light".

Now that was the important detail she missed. But I was very thankful for her help,"That'll be very much helpful. But I wanted to know one more thing. Why did you insisted on coming? Why not William and the others?"

She was startled by my question but composed herself as she nodded at her mate, "Because I wanted to meet you," the wolfman said "I am Alpha Ryan Greyhound, Alpha of Night Shade pack".

I was confused at this werewolf whom I don't even know and never met, "What would you have with me?" I asked him.

"We had an elder in our pack who died a few months ago. He carried a big secret which he revealed to me on his deathbed after hiding so many centuries."

"Is it related to me?"

"Yes. The elder was previously with Blood Moon pack in other continent. He was already old when he joint our pack after his was wiped out by the Valacs. The attack on Valaacs a few centuries ago was schemed by his alpha. He was the sole survivor of that battle. His pack was manipulated against their will into killing all the Valac children"

"Against their will?"

"Yes...more like compulsion or hypnosis but an extremely strong kind of...Such powers are only harbored by the vampires or witches. He didn't give any name just kept on saying 'Silver Cross'. At that time, the Reese, Gregors, and Bloodstones all had their moonstones. So who exactly was the mastermind and what was his motive I don't know? But I thought maybe I should warn you. Now to believe it or not is up to you. The other Valacs are cruel and you are the only better from that bunch since you have your humanity from your mother..."

My mind was frozen still by what I just heard. My parents, my grandpa, my uncle and aunt all were killed. Uptil now everyone thought it was those wolves but it was not. I can't even think its Matilda or John because this incident happened even before the Bloodstone massacre. It only means someone else. Who might it be...

I have to keep it secret from everyone until I get my answers," Does William and the others know this?"

"No I didn't said it to anyone. Only you two know and I wont tell anyone else. You have my word" Ryan replied with sincerity in his eyes. I nodded and we took our leave. I checked my phone and went towards our jet. I should call William...

Claude: I don't think I can reach for the party. We are late. Will be there by early morning. Is Serena ok?

William: Yes. She's having dinner with Charles. She's fine...

Claude: Ok. Please look at her. I'll be back soon...

I missed the dance with her. I just hope to reach home soon at least I can see her in gown.

Unknown POV

Serena was nowhere to be found. The last I saw her she was eating with that brat. Suddenly I felt two manas going crazy on the first floor. It was those two vampire Kings. Crazy bastards...Whats with them now. I tried to overhear the conversation but the loud music was irritating so I went and hid in a room on the first floor. Those dickheads are so slow they cant even make out I am a human or vampire. I masked my mana so flawlessly.

"I don't feel good. I feel angry and fear for some reason...Something's not correct"

"Me too...Its the same like last time when we went at feu follet. I just can't control now. Michael you need to evacuate everyone out before we loose control"

Why the fuck did this mutts went to feu follet. And why are they panicking like rabid dogs. Suddenly I heard a fire alarm, a fake one of course and everyone downstairs panicked and cleared out. The wolves and vampires knew it wasn't fire but something else but still they cleared.

"Wait...Where's Serena?"

"Oh No....Where is she? Charles she was with you right" a woman asked the brat.

"She went to the restroom"

"Ok...Somebody go and get her else she'll evacuate with the others"

These fucktards...I immediately left and searched for her scent. I couldn't smell her anywhere. Not even among the humans. Her scent ended in washroom. All cubicles door were open. At this point, I dint care a damn that I am in ladies restroom. I just needed to search her. I was very nervous where she might be. I came out realizing soon someone would reach here to search for her.

A faint smell led me to the terrace. Why did she went there? I followed it. I didn't see her anywhere. But the scent was stronger as I came close. The animal inside me was taking over by that strong smell,the smell of fresh blood,her blood.

I panicked hoping she is fine until my eyes fell on a golden bracelet and few drops of her blood. The thought of her being hurt enraged me. I knew she was wounded but nowhere found. The trail of her scent took me towards the railing and disappeared. I looked down and found nothing but gushing water. Without wasting a moment I dived in...

Claude's POV

The logical traitor would be Vincent's father Markus. May be for the throne but still I don't see it possible. He didnt had the power to compel instead he had telekinesis. And he loved his brothers more than anything even though he didnt like me or my mother. So it can't be him.

Markus striked off...

Vincent's mother Diana might be the one. She might have wanted her husband or her child on the throne. But she had ability to create lightning. Also she's a coward I can't think of her pulling out something like this on her own.

Diana striked off...

Vincent the most cruel of all Valacs and probably he would have even attempted to do this if he was born then...

Vincent striked off...

I cant imagine William or his family doing this. Loyalty runs in their blood in all of them. It can never be them.

Gregors striked off...

Ivan's mother might be. She's one power-hungry woman. She wanted to marry Zephyr's father but why would she lead the attack that too with the help of werewolves and that doesnt explain why she would want to kill me then. Also I remember Ivan saying she had ability to create storms no compulsion...But still she has a motive

Queen Evelyn suspect...

Matilda and John were laying low that time . They attacked the Reese and Gregors almost 200 years after the werewolf attack. And I dont think they would go only after the Valac children. Their main target was the moonstones not us.

Matilda & John striked off

The Bloodstones might be the one. But what would be their motive to just kill the Valac children. I have no idea what powers or abilities they possessed but they might have had hidden motive. Though I can't go and kill them since they're all dead but still it can be them.

Bloodstones suspect

The council might want to rule but why just the Valac kids why not Reese, Bloodstones and Gregors. I'm sure Claire and Isaac were born then why not them. And as everyone know Ions have best abilities and powers. So it must be someone from them.

Council suspect

My mind was going crazy thinking all the people I suspected. Even if it were not one of them and someone else who would it be. I'll take it slow and investigate later once my love is out of danger. My prime focus is her now. I have to protect her now instead of crying on what I already lost.

The jet was about to land near the mansion. I glanced Levi who was sitting with Rose's picture the whole time. I always use to feel it funny and use to mock him but now that I had fallen in love myself I realize how love changes you as a person. He kept the picture in his bag and said, "We're here".

I was so lost in my thoughts I didn't realized we already landed. The sun started to peek from the clouds and darkness was slowly disappearing. We stepped down and went inside. Finally, I can see her...

Everyone was still in their party attires. Ivan and the witches were present as well. Everyone looked tensed. William was moving back and forth in the hallway whereas Ivan was kneeling down with his hands on his head. Charles had red swollen eyes as if he just cried. Something bad must've happened at the party. As soon as their eyes fell on me, there faces were filled with terror. Everyone went into an alert mode.

My eyes surveyed the faces but Serena was not there and her scent it was missing,"Where is Serena?" I asked glaring at William.

William had a serious look on his face. He took a step forward and said, "She escaped".

"What do you mean escape?" I roared in anger causing everyone to flinch in their positions taking defensive stances.

Cassandra stepped in front of William abnd said, "Something happened at the party. She went to the restroom and then nobody saw her. It was indeed a big mistake we trusted her with freedom and this is how she repaid us. All what we found was this on terrace near the railing. She jumped off into the river and escaped. We tried to find her in the river but we couldn't..." she handed a golden bracelet towards me. The same braclet which I gifted her which had stains of her blood on it. I couldn't bring myself to believe she was no longer with me. She left me.

"No way...She can never jump on her own" Levi screamed and looked me and said "She can't swim...".

"May be she lied you Levi" I heard Cecily hissing...

By this moment, I lost my temper completely. All I could see was red...

I lost her

She left me

The only person who really made me feel alive was not there

I felt dead

I felt broken

Anger

Grief

Pain

Rage

Everthing was Red....It was all Blood

Darkness consumed me...The monster inside me was pushing itself over...

I couldn't see anything else.....

Chapter 23 – New Life

Unknown POV

The water flowed at a rapid pace. It was very difficult for me to get her scent in the water unless she's bleeding. I swam towards the rocks but couldn't see anything other than marine vegetation.

Suddenly, my nose caught a faint scent of blood that flowed towards the direction of the water. I swam tearing through the massive waves as fast as I could. The scent went stronger with every stroke. I stopped near the roots of a huge tree and got out of water. The scent was strongest here and blood was all in the air. She was hurt.

Serena, Please be ok...

Every second felt so long. My anxiety was killing me inside. This monstrous river and her scent was driving me insane. I just hope she's safe...

I sniffed the area and ended near a big rock. I saw a pool of blood near the rock. I wonder how she managed to swim past this monstrous river. But I am glad she's out.

I tried to follow her scent but it was not there. How is this possible? She has to have a scent if she walks past from here or if anyone saved her. But I couldn't get any other person's scent as well. I am losing my mind now. Even this blood is fresh but I can't sense her at all anywhere. With the amount of blood that is lying here, she can't walk by herself she must be unconscious. Did someone took her...

I searched the forest nearby.

No scents...

No manas...

No humans...

Not even any damn footprints...

Nothing just nothing...

Where did you go...

SERENA...

Serena's POV

'Why did you bring her here Sussane. We should leave her in a human settlement'

'She has two manas. And she is human. She must be someone special'

'She's very beautiful. Let's keep her here.'

'Keep your hands away from her Resmelda. And Sussane, why did you go to that party in the first place'

'I wanted to see Malcolm. Also, we won't leave her anywhere. Charles seemed to be friends with her and so did the Gregors and Reese. Hilda please...'

'Yes Hilda Please let me keep her'

'She's heavily bleeding and I'm going to lose my control now if she's not treated asap. Mary can you treat her wounds'

'Yes Hilda'

I heard a few females in the background but my sight was blurry and my head was pounding. I tried to open my eyes but they felt very heavy. Darkness was itching to consume me in its cloak. I tried to fight but it eventually won.

***

I woke up to find myself in a small cabin-like room. The walls were wooden and so was the ceiling. It felt like I was inside a tree-house. There was a large glass window. The view was mesmerizing. The mountains were stretched in different shades of blue and darkness was slowly taking control.

I am not in Gregors palace. Where am I?

I checked myself being covered with a woolen blanket. I got terrified seeing myself naked under the sheets a few bandages covered my arms, knees and head. I held the sheet close to me and covered myself. My eyes surveyed desperately to find some clothes but there was nothing. I tried to sit up but my body didn't support me.

"Awake?" a woman with black long hair and black eyes said nonchalantly entering the room. She wore a plain white dress. Three more women followed her. All of them had the same black hair and black eyes. They all had similar characteristic brownish tanned skin. All of them were dressed very simple in similar white dresses. One of them had a necklace made of beads and conches who seemed in her late twenties. She looked very pretty and had a big smile on her face. She smiled at me and tried to come close but another girl stopped her. She seemed younger than the rest of them around my age. The other two women look in their late thirties.

"Where am I? Who are you?" I asked softly. For some reason, I wasn't scared of them. Though I didn't know them I assumed they saved me and treated me.

"My name is Hilda. This is Sussane. She saved you when you were drowning" the woman in white pointed towards the little girl before continuing "Who are you?"

"My name's Serena" my voice sounded weak and sleepy.

"What were you doing with Charles?" the girl in the beaded necklace said. The smile on her face was turned to a serious expression.

The question surprised me. How did she know him? I wonder if these people are vampires as well. They look normal humans to me.

They don't look bad people. But if they're humans and they ask me about Charles what should I say. Will they cause him any harm. Though they look harmless but still...

Seeing me not replying to Sussane spoke, "I saw you with Charles and also with the Gregors and Reese Kings. She was pretty friendly with William as well". Sussane talked as if accusing me of something. She narrowed her eyes towards me whereas the other girl seemed restless. I just didn't know how to answer her.

" Uh...um...They're just friends" I mumbled not willing to give out any secrets about their existence.

"Well, your heart is going to pop out at any moment. Never mind. Mary..." she called a tall woman who had a serious look as she approached towards me. Mary placed her hand on my wrist and closed her eyes. I was hesitant but she had an iron grip on my hand. Her touch was cold...like ice...like death. She was one of them...She was a vampire...They all are vampires.

Everyone stared at us waiting for the verdict. Are they going to kill me now? These women saved my life haven't attacked me yet. And they look pretty harmless but still...

"She is a part of the prophecy and would help the two kings to get their moonstones back. Apparently, as per feu follet, Matilda had masked her with her mana which they plan on removing by making her drink the blood of her guardians" Mary announced and everyone was shocked. Their eyes widened at the information.

"If her guardians are wolves then it won't be an issue. But if they are vampires then it cannot be removed so easily. If she drinks a vampire's blood she would turn into one and then they can't get their moonstones back if she's impure. What was that spirit even thinking..." Hilda sounded frustrated and angry as well. The others kept their gazes down as if they were scared of her.

"Maybe the medium who asked her didn't have enough mana so they might not have full information..." Mary murmured.

"Ya, that would be the case. The spirit never lies...Anyways, we need to keep this human here with us. Finally, there is some peace in all these centuries. With the two main families not having their powers, a war can be avoided. We just need to protect as many lives as we can even if it mean the Valacs being superpowers" Hilda announced. Her eyes stayed focused on the other three women. The other women nodded with determination.

Am I being held a hostage? Am I again being kidnapped? My eyes welled with tears at the thought of how they would treat me now.

"Don't cry. Nobody here would hurt you" the girl with beaded necklace stepped forward and wiped my tears. She smiled warmly towards me and kissed the back of my hand. I flinched at her sudden gesture.

She let out a chuckle ,"My name is Resmelda. You would be staying here with us. We are vampires but we won't drink from you so you don't have to be worried or scared love. I'll take care of you". The way she said seem very weird.

Mary cleared her throat while Sussane kept a tray in front of me which had a few apples and berries and a grilled fish. "For now this all we have. Mary might go to the village and stock up some food by tomorrow".

I nodded. She got me all this forest products and I was glad for it. The women left my room but Resmelda stayed seated there. "Let me help".

She cut it all in small pieces and fed me. I looked outside the window. It was almost dark now. My thoughts drifted to Claude. Will he notice I went missing? Will he try to search me? But who was the one who tried to kill me? And what does he want with me and who are these women...

***

Two months have passed since I came here. Resmelda was the only one who use to talk to me like a normal person. The others never even attempted to start any conversation apart from Sussane who asked me about William's uncle Malcolm on first day. But alas I had never ever seen him nor did I knew anything about him.

I got to know from Resmelda that she was Hilda's younger sister. They stayed together in forest for a long time away from other vampires. And at some point, Mary and Sussane came to stay with them together who were their cousins. They were all females and had absolute hatred towards men.

They occasionally went to the city for some work. Although she didn't tell me for what and I didn't dare to ask. When returning they use to bring few clothes, toiletries and other essentials for me. Sometimes I used to wonder where did they get the money for all this. But they still lived a simple life in forest. Seeing them, I also asked Resmelda to stop bringing me fancy clothes. I only accepted a few undergarments but I wore the same plain white clothes these women use to wear.

Resmelda or sometimes Mary use to do my hairs in a dutch-braid or a halo-braid. Sussane didn't talk much and Hilda most of time use to meditate. So did the others. Apparently, it helps them control their mana and makes them powerful. I saw them doing it for almost 3-4 hours everyday but Hilda use to do it like more than ten hours. No doubt she was powerful.

I spent my time in cleaning the house, gathering berries and getting fish and fresh water everyday from the lake. I never tried to escape because these people treated me nicely and I was allowed to roam around as I wished. We stayed in the middle of forest. I knew it was somewhere very very far from Gregors place.

The forest around Gregors were filled with tall conical vegetation but the forest here was very lush green and thick with abundant resources. Even if Mary didn't bring food from the village, anyone can survive here with all the natural products.

The four women stayed all alone here. I never saw them drinking any blood from any humans or even from blood-pouches. They didn't even had a refrigerator. I assumed they might have some contract-humans or something. I never asked them, I didn't even wanted to know.

I sat near the rocks and slowly immersed myself in the water uptil my waist. Resmelda stayed out near a tree staring me as usual. She use to bring me to the waterfall for a bath every alternate day. The waterfall was small but serene and the water was crystal-clear. The white water cascaded down a series of rocky outcrops, giving the effect of many waterfalls rather than just one. No matter how many times I came here, every time I felt very excited. I was enjoying my new life here.

Unknown POV"You have to go. You had missed it enough times already but not now" Kyle said in an authoritative tone. Did he forget who he is talking to. I glanced at him and he immediately stole his eyes away.

"I have some important things to do" I spatted and took my glass of blood-wine.

"I've been observing you from a month. Where do you go everyday. Seems something interesting...Or rather someone interesting" the red-haired prick smirked at me while Kyle kept his eyes glued on mine. Scott was quick witted and stronger than his father. He knew I am upto something and had started to doubt. I don't want him to know at any cost about where I am going...about Serena...

"Brother, why don't you stop bothering my prince and get your ass out of here", the other red-haired came running towards me and clunged to my arm pouting at her brother. Unlike her brother, she was a dim-wit but still strong. Of all the ions, these twins were strongest. If anyone is a real match to my strength it would be Scott. He has his remarkable abilities and also strength. The ions are trying to get Scarlett marry me so that they would have a better control over the Valacs. But I don't want to. I already have my eyes set on someone. And she will be the one...No, she has to be the one...

I gulped the glasses down my throat. I don't want to witness those idiots demonstrating their non-existing strength just showing off Vincent and whoever it is. All I want to do is find her. But I have to go that day else these bastards would start suspecting me. I need to go there.

"Fine. When is it?" I muttered clearly expressing my annoyance.

"In two weeks. You need to go in disguise and mask your mana" Kyle stated.

He didn't need to say that. These buffoons didn't know I always keep my guard up unlike them. I always mask my mana and go everywhere in disguise. If I were to release my mana, this dunces would have went crazy. Bloody morons...

Chapter 24 – Preparations

Claude's POV

"North is clear. Nobody saw her. We couldn't trace her" Levi replied and again we met a dead end. Its been two months now she's missing. Every second without her feels like I'm dying again and again. This death is never-ending. I know she's alive. Cassandra has even confirmed the same but nobody's able to find her.

"Don't worry Claude. We will find her. And whoever is behind all this, I'll make sure he dies a painful death" William assured me. He sat infront of me with his hands on his head. He felt very guilty since I left my Serena in his care before she went missing. Since that day he's searching for her every day with Ivan. I'm happy both of them turned out to be her guardians and not some wolves. All what we need now is to get her back.

We searched in all directions all over the continent but couldn't find her which is highly impossible with so many vampires finding her together. It feels like she's with someone stronger, someone powerful enough to hide her so effectively. I just hope it's not those evil siblings or the council.

Eva was in deep thought swirling her finger through her hairs. Levi was as usual gaping at Rose like a love-sick puppy. Rose was sipping her wine with Charles and other girls. Cassie and William both sat at the dining table tensed. For Cassie, I knew she cared only to get the moonstones back, not about my Serena, but William truly cared for her and now that I know he's the guardian, I'm relieved seeing him fine. It means wherever Serena is, she's not in danger. He took whole bottle of blood-wine and gulped it down through his throat in frustration. He blamed himself for all this.

Even Ivan had changed. He has been finding her day and night since he found he was her guardian. But I decided, after today I'll call off the search for her and will search myself using some other ways. These whole two months everyone was spending their time only to look for her and it was out of fear, of my wrath. I have another way to search for her but I want it to be last resort.

Cassie was going through Aradia's book, flipping pages after pages, but still no use.

William was just continuously calling his kindred asking for updates. But no use.

I saw Jared coming in the main hall along with a few vampires. His blue shirt was tainted with blood. He quickly ran towards Rose. Whenever I see them together, I feel this pang of jealousy in my heart. I wanted what they had for myself with my Serena. I felt bad for poor Levi. He was hopelessly in love with Rose. All these years, I never saw him with any other female. He had his eyes set only on her.

"He's coming..." Jared informed.

What the...I didn't sense that bastard. He might have masked his mana. I just want to kill him for how he dared to touch my love. How dare he put his filthy hands on her delicate skin. He deserved to die and I will kill that m*therf*cker today.

My temper was rising slowly and I could see everyone being cautious and stepping away from me. Fear was evident on their faces. William ran towards Charles and hugged him tightly. I saw Rose was being tucked protectively behind Jared and Levi stood in front of them both. Even he was scared, of my anger, for the beast I had turned into. "Claude, you need to control your anger. We know he was wrong but he's an ion, that too a prince. We need his help right now. He's the only one from council who can help us. We cannot hurt him. Are you even listening?" William snapped me out of my anger, "We need his help to find her...You need to calm down".

The other vampires already fled from the scene. Eva and Charles were nowhere to be seen. Only William, Levi and Jared stood there with Cassandra who was quivering behind William. I cannot blame her. She was terrified of me now after I unleashed my wrath, my true powers, my new abilities. By this time, all the furniture was levitating in the air, the windows were shattered. The ground was shaking in horror. The tremors were felt by the objects which were still on the ground and ready to levitate in air.

" So the rumors were true then" the red-haired bastard entered the mansion with Cecily. He had an evil glint in his eyes, "The flightless bird can actually fly" he continued mocking me.

" Scott, don't provoke him unless you don't value your life" William warned him pointing towards the rubble of the eastern tower which I obliterated in my frenzy two months back. Now there was only debris. The sight was a constant reminder of the monster I am...

"Woah... Some crazy ability you have there. Might I know, why am I being called here and why this vampire is fuming over me" he talked to William pointing towards me. My rage hung to my patience by a thread. I was this close to destroy him. But William glanced me with his pleading eyes to keep calm.

William quickly started explaining him the situation,"Serena is missing. Our vampires searched all over the continent. She was not found. No trace. She went missing from Michael's party. No scent, no mana was found near her blood. Also, we had confirmed she's not dead. The only one capable to do this are ions. All we want to know from you is whether the council has her or not" .

Scott's expression was completely changed. The smug look on his face disappeared and filled by a stunned expression. His eyes widened at the revelation, "No. That's not possible. The council don't have any idea of her existence. Did you guys even searched properly?" He paced to and fro and took a seat on the couch which was now broken. The rest of furniture was scattered around upside down, some broken and some overlapped on each other. I couldn't make out why was he so shocked at this revelation.

"You won't leave alive out of here if you don't spit out truth. Where is she?" I threatened him while he smirked at me.

"What's his problem?" he asked William and got up from the couch while anger flashed on his face, "Don't forget I am the prince and also a part of the council and what are you? A banished prince. I wouldn't even call you a prince. If you attack me, you all are getting doomed. I had come here to help only because Cecily asked me to. The council doesn't have the little butterfly, that's for sure I can say. Why don't you go and ask your brother or your uncle then? Or may be she got captured again by the Bloodstone witch or having a good time with the werewolves for all you know", he snapped at me.

Little butterfly? What the fuck did he call my love? Yes she is a butterfly, a delicate little one but this bastard have no right to call her that. I clenched my fist in anger and was about to say but William fumed, "Don't step over your limits Scott. I am not listening a word against Claude. Before we lose our calm, leave".

He let out a sigh, "I merely stated facts. I just wished I was the one to ravish the beautiful flower...".

Thats it.

The thread of my patience was cut off and my blood lust was taking over.

"You bastard", I threw a punch on him and his body rammed on the wall. Before I could lay another killing blow, a voice stopped me.

"Stop it".

We all turned to find out Ada. She had a serious expression as usual and Ivan stood next to her. "Calm down Claude. We don't want the whole council running for our heads. Its no use to hit him. He speaks truth. I can sense. The council doesn't have her" Ada continued as she entered.

Ivan glanced in disgust and anger at the bastard who was now getting dirt out of his body and continued, "Currently, we are helpless because whoever has her must be super strong. And they are definitely not werewolves else we could have sniffed them. Its either those evil siblings or someone stronger. As of now, the ones I know who could conceal their mana so skillfully are only ions. None of us present here can do that with so much precision. It has to be ions. Someone from the council..." he stated contradicting Ada. But who might it be. I have recently gained my abilities, stronger than these people but even I cannot mask my mana as ingeniously as it was done at the sight of her blood.

Scott came forward and I clenched my fist and was ready to throw another punch if he speak any more shit, "Well there must be some trick behind it or its also possible the little butterfly was hiding her true talents uptil now and escaped the first chance she got".

This bastard...

Ivan narrowed his eyes at Scott and asked, "What about Zephyr?" The smirk on his face vanished and he defensively replied, "What about him?"

The sudden change of expression confirmed there is something about him. If not related to Serena then something else. I must say Ivan was very cunning and smart to catch him off-guard like this. They're definitely hiding something. "Do you take us all for fools. He was hidden all these centuries and now he suddenly shows up but still staying with the council instead of Valacs. He might be the one..."

Scott laughed hysterically, "Why would he do that? He doesn't even know the butterfly". And it was a fact. I turned to Ada and she nodded. He was telling the truth. Then what is the council hiding.

Ivan continued, "You would never know. Why don't you tell us all about him?"

Scott continued laughing like a mad-man, "You don't have to wait long. He would be soon making his appearance in BlackSun festival."

***

Only one day is left for BlackSun. No sign of Serena. No leads, no clues...I just miss her so much. I walked out of my room and saw Rose and Jared making out on the couch. My eyes went to dining table next to the couch. William was casually sipping his blood wine without a care about the couple making out in front of him. This man...

"Get a room" Cassandra snapped at them entering the hall. She saw me walking dowstairs and left the room. They stopped kissing and steadied their clothes and watched me. Rose's cheeks flushed red on her pale skin. She look very adorable but not more than my love.

"Hey" William waived at me.

"Hey, did you see Levi" I asked.

"Nope. I was thinking of something" he said looking in my eye. He took a deep breath and continued, "There's only one more powerful witch we know who can help us. Crystal... We can get her to feu-follet and ask Serena's whereabouts".

The hell...Why didn't I think of that. I met Crystal. She's a very friendly person and I'm sure she would never reject me. "Ya...Why didn't I think of that. Lets go asap".

He said, "No. Not now. Tomorrow is BlackSun. We will leave after that. Are you going to participate?".

I didn't want to. I don't want to show-off my new found power to anyone neither was I interested in that stupid bloody battle, "No, are you going to participate?".

"Not at all. All my kindred are eager to put their strength to test this year. So it would be very unfair that I took part and they all lose", he smirked and continued drinking.

Serena's POV

"BlackSun festival?" I asked Resmelda while she was sparring with Sussane. She landed a swift blow right on her face. Sussane's nose was bleeding but it stopped in a few seconds. Both of them were panting now. Their clothes torn and bodies covered with dirt.

Sussane left the ground and Resme came and sat next to me, "Its a festival every vampire is supposed to attend no matter age or social status. It is held once a century. The council holds it at the Valacs palace from last six centuries. Prior to that, it was rotationally taking place at each of four royal houses. But with all three of them losing their moonstones, now its held with Valacs. It is a very important festival for vampires. Each vampire is supposed to attend it, if they value their lives", she replied drinking something from her black bottle. It was definitely blood but I didn't ask.

"What do you mean"

She wiped her mouth with a black cloth and shoved the bottle inside her dress,"It takes place on a very rare solar eclipse hence the name 'BlackSun'. The power emmiting from the eclipse falls on the stone and all the vampires in the vicinity rejuvenates themselves with new life force. Vampires are not immortal as you think. Whoever is not present at this time near the stone, dies."

This was a very shocking revelation to me. All this time, I thought they just drink blood and stay immortal. So they have to anyhow get this once every hundred years to live the next hundred. So much for a living, "Oh...So you also will go?"

She smiled at me and tossed my hairs placing a kiss on my cheek, "Yes we have to. Its a great time to know about everyone else. There are fights and battle royales. Its very interesting. Though, Hilda never allow us to participate but its great to watch. You'll also come with us this time."

I asked in confused, "Me?"

"Yes, you too. Don't worry nobody would know. We have a trick up our sleeves. Also, we can't leave you here all alone" She smiled at me carrying me bridal style and within few second we were back to the cabin.

I entered my room and watched through the window while having fruits. All the women were meditating deeply. I've been observing them from last two weeks. Day by day they are meditating for longer durations. It was as though they were preparing themselves for a battle...

***

Chapter 25 - BlackSun

The clear lake mirrored our reflection. I found this entire get-up a little uncanny. All of us look quintuplets with identical white cloaks. I wore the white mask which covered my nose and mouth. Apparently, Resmelda and the others had the ability to completely conceal mana. According to her, everyone would think I am a vampire and not a human. And I was strictly told not to leave their side even for a moment. Not that I was planning to. I had adapted to their way of living and I was happy with it. I wanted to see Claude and the others as well but I knew I didn't belong in their life. I wanted them to have moonstones but Hilda said it would lead to a war and I didn't want the burden of so many lives on my head. So I decided to live some time here and Hilda promised she would leave me safely among humans when everything is sorted.

"No matter what, don't leave my side", Hilda warned again for the third time and I nodded. We reached the main entrance of the big arena. There were two massive iron gates with a half-moon sign crested on each. I saw a few vampires outside the arena talking to each other in groups. As soon as they saw us, they stopped talking and continued staring at us. I felt a bit self-conscious with so many judgemental eyes gaping us. Everyone was either in their combat suits, sportswear, tracksuits, and some even in casual jeans and tees. We were the only five in white dresses and white cloaks. I wonder if we look like freaks. Paranoia was taking over slowly. What if I get caught. Resmelda sensed it and slightly pressed my arm to comfort me. A gatekeeper handed us a band which we were supposed to wear on our left hand. We wore it and left in.

As soon as we took our seats, Hilda and Mary sat to my right, and Resmelda and Sussane sat to my left. The arena was circular with numerous pillars marked with numbers. There was a stage on the right side of the arena which had people who were dressed like royals.

"Those are the Valacs. The one with the crown is the current King Vincent" Resmelda whispered.

Claude's brother

He looked young compared to William and Claude. He was extremely fair and good-looking. He didn't had the overly muscular body like Claude but I could see he was fit and had a lean body.

"And to his right are his parents, the previous king and queen. The one in black suit is his advisor Liam. He is stronger than the king himself. To his left, the woman in black gown is his witch, Felicia. She's the most powerful witch among all the witches till date. I think maybe more powerful than Matilda but I am not completely sure" she said pointing the short-haired petite woman who looks in her late thirties. "Then there are other Valacs next to them, their relatives and their distant cousins. Big family..."

All the Valacs looked scary and screamed authority. My eyes scanned the arena and landed on Ivan. He was sitting in what seemed like a private area sipping wine. Ivan's mother and Irene sat there along with their coterie. A similar VIP area was next to this one. William and the others were present there. My eyes stayed focused on Claude as he was talking something with William and soon their eyes settled near us. I quickly stole my eyes away from him and gazed down.

The whole arena was filled. I never thought there might be so many vampires. I think practically all the vampires of the world were present here. Luckily, we were not the only ones with masks. There were a few men as well as women who covered their faces but still in combat suits. I wonder why. "Why do some of them are covering their faces?" I asked.

"Some vampires don't want their identity to be disclosed. Some have hidden powers, some are rogues, some are even enemies to the Valacs. Hence, they cover their faces and mask their manas while fighting here" she replied.

Suddenly, there was complete silence all over. And the king started speaking,

"Hello everyone, I welcome you all here to celebrate 'BlackSun'. Like every time, this century as well we would have the tournament. There's only a small twist for this century to make this day memorable for everyone present here. I want it to be etched in golden words into the history of vampires and I feel proud to see that I would be the one holding this. Liam...", he motioned his advisor sitting on his right. The man took a torch of fire and lit it. A girl who was dressed like a maid took Felicia's hand and helped her stand. She carfeully directed the petite witch next to the Liam.

Felicia is blind...

Everyone seemed confused as to what is happening. I could see some people whispering, others seemed panicked. "What happen? What's going on?" I asked Resmelda.

"I don't know what's happening" Resmelda replied in a terrified voice. Though I couldn't see her expression, her wavering voice seemed tense. Liam gave the torch to Felicia and moved away. Everyone else moved away from Felicia as she murmured something and the flame distributed into several splinters and flew all across the arena. One of the splinters landed on my left wrist on the band which was given by the gatekeeper. The band started glowing red. Resmelda panicked seeing me so did Hilda and others. All across the arena, there were many vampires who had their bands glowing.

I looked at Resmelda's wrist, her's didn't glow.

Neither Mary's...

Nor Hilda's...

Nor Sussane's...

Only mine glowed...

"Every century, many vampires hide their true strength and the event gets boring. So this year, I had Felicia to set this up. Those who have their bands glowing have to participate mandatorily and the winner would be awarded whatever his wish is, if that is something me or my witch can fulfill. The rules are simple. Either kill the other vampire or remove their bands. No-one can use their special abilities because the ring is enchanted. You need to use your raw muscle-power. And no-one can forfeit the fight ", the king announced and sat on his throne.

I awaited Hilda's next command but only horror could be seen in those black eyes of hers as one by one the red bands came on the central fighting grounds.

***

William's POV

"What the hell is this" Levi bursted in anger. He was willing to participate but was not chosen. On the other hand, I was worried about Rose. She was not a fighter. She was initially a human and was a very weak vampire. She was very scared. I could see the fear on her face. But I was glad at least Jared was there with her. And so was Cecily and some others from my coterie. All my kindreds went to the grounds.

I saw Ivan's coterie. He too was not chosen. His butler Martin, Irene, and his cousin Leila were chosen along with a few others I didn't knew. They went to the arena. All of them were strong and they fearlessly went to the grounds. I saw Nicolas from the Valacs also descending the royal stage and joining the grounds.

There were around 100 vampires selected. Some look scared and some look very happy to be chosen. It's going to be a bloody battle. I just hope my people come out safe. Everyone was full set and ready to attack. A brunette in a white cloak caught my attention. She had a white mask on her face. All I could see were her brown eyes. Probably a rogue...

"How is she going to fight in a dress?" I murmured. Claude laughed, "Probably she never imagined herself on that part of the arena".

"Ya...But she looks so scared. Hopefully, she gets defeated not killed", I said feeling pity for the brunette.

"This is not fair. Some of us wanted to participate. We waited for nearly a century for this festival and now we can't even participate to prove ourselves. You need to change the rules" a man from what I assumed was a rogue spouted in anger, gaining everyone's attention. Many people encouraged him and the arguments increased by the second.

Vincent motioned Liam and whispered something in his ear. Liam stood and announced, "Ok. Sounds fair. The king has allowed anyone who wishes to participate. However, one who is already chosen by the flame cannot back out. Only those from the viewers who wish to join can participate. And the kings of the royal family cannot enter the fight. Now those who wish to enter may join in."

"I would participate", a husky voice came from the crowds, and then when I saw who it belonged to, fury overtook my senses. It was Rowan. He never ever participated in these tournaments all these centuries. Why now? He took part only once, seven centuries back when 'BlackSun' was held with the Reese family. He misbehaved with my Claire and groped some females in the ring. Bloody pervert.

But he killed many males and almost killed Ivan's elder brother Isaac, just because he tried to save Claire. The bastard entered the ground and stood there. All the vampires who were cheering earlier, including the rogue who asked to change the rules, stay glued to their seats, seeing Rowan entering the fight. Nobody dared to enter and now I was very much worried about my kindred.

Levi stepped down and entered the ring as well. All the eyes were on him. At the same time, I saw Ria from the ions moving towards the ring. She was already in her combat suit with a sinister smile. I could hear people whispering each other about how these two are going to get killed by Rowan. A muscular man in jet black hair also jumped the same time and landed in the middle. He wore jeans and a t-shirt, not even a combat suit but his overall appearance screamed dominance though his personality appeared very absent-minded and negligent. I'm sure he's hiding his true mana under the pretence of being an air-head. Who is he? I never ever saw him? Might be some newly turned vampire or a rogue...

Suddenly, silence crept over the whole arena pulling me out of my thoughts. I looked everyone around me and they all gaped in a particular direction. Four women in white cloaks and their faces covered with white masks entered the ring. All the eyes were on these enig-matic women who were cutting across the flood of vampires. The vampires were even parting way for them. All of them had similar clothing like the brunette who was chosen. Seeing them, felt like they are part of some cult. They made their way towards the brunette who was chosen and surrounded her protectively from all four sides. They are guarding their friend. Unlike the scared girl, these women look strong and confident. They all had long black hair, unlike their brunette friend who was cowering with fear in the center.

Liam broke the silence, "I assume everyone's here now. Felicia you can start..."

Felicia chanted a spell and the ring was covered in a translucent barrier while Liam continued, "Nobody from outside can enter the ring. And nobody from inside can exit, unless they die, or their band is removed, or he or she is the winner. Now, let the Battle Royale begin".It was chaos. All I could hear was gushing of wind and heart-piercing screams. The air smelled like blood. The dirt besieged the ring like an envelope of dust forming a small tornado which is possible if someone is moving in circular motion with an immense speed. I couldn't see for few minutes what was occurring behind that whirlwind of air and filth. Some vampires came out flying from the ring and settled on their seat. One of my kindred Sam also came flying and was settled on the seat. I quickly went towards him, " What happened in there?"

His face was filled with horror and his clothes were bloody, " I have no idea. I couldn't even see who took my band off. But whichever vampire it was, was superfast. Nobody saw him. I don't even fucking know if it was a he or a she. Whoever it was, was not Rowan that I am sure of. Rowan was on his killing spree. He killed many vampires all males but this vampire who removed our band was certainly not him. It felt as if he's saving us by quickly removing us all from the ring. I feel so pathetic now." I could see unshed tears in his eyes filled with terror.

Soon, the dirt settled on the ground and the view was clear. The ring was all clear. Approximately, thirty vampires still stood there. Around ten vampires laid lifeless on the ground. All males. Their hearts were ripped out and kept on their stomach. Their bodies laid in a line.

Bloody Rowan...

I saw corpses of two females with many cuts on their faces and their hairs in their mouth. This could only be that twisted bastard Rowan. I didn't knew how could he stoop so low. Both girls were very young.

Son of a b*tch...

If whatever Sam said was true, the superfast vampire whoever it was, in a way he saved many lives by defeating them as soon as possible. The only vampires standing now were all the powerful bunch, that was clear now and were fighting one-on-one.

Martin was fighting with Nicolas. Nicolas punched him but Martin dodged it. Nicolas sped up his heavy punches and kept punching till he was unconscious. When he laid still on the ground, he kicked him in his gut and removed his band. Martin came flying towards Reese's area and was still unconscious.

My eyes went to Rowan who cornered two females. One of them was probably rogue and the other was from the council. Both looked very weak and were wincing with terror. He held them both in each of his arms and drag them towards him, "So kittens, tell me you wanna play with me or scratch me. He laid a trail of kisses on both their necks.

But suddenly, his sight was caught by another group. He removed the bands of his captives and moved towards his new prey.

It was a girl wearing a 'V mask' popularly known as Guy Fawkes mask fighting with Ivan's kindred. They all stood in a protective formation around Irene who laid unconscious. Ivan looked very tensed. I know it must be very hard for him to see his sister all bloody and bruised. I was more worried about the 'V mask girl' who was clearly focused on anyhow getting her hands on Irene ignoring all others around her. If I remember correctly, the 'V mask' was a symbol of 'vendetta'. Does she crave some sort of revenge or is it mere coincidence. She circled around the formation and the next moment, she threw all the five hearts she had collected leaving the dead bodies on the ground.

Ruthless...

Strong...

I saw Ivan stood up and so did his mother. They were terrified of what was going to happen to Irene who laid unconscious and vulnerable on the ground. Soon, an unexpected person comes to her rescue...

Rowan...

"Not so fast love..." he held the 'V-mask' girl by her wrist. The girl didn't reply and struggled to get out of his clutches. She did a quick somersault and moved away from the two. This girl...She's very strong. Rowan stayed guarding Irene.

"I can't let you kill this flower here, else my friend Ada would be very upset. Why don't you just give up on her and lets have a good time" he smirked at the girl but the girl moved with a supersonic speed and planted a kick on his face.

Damn. That pervert deserved it

"Feisty here, aren't we", he smirked and moved towards her, "but I like the submissive types" . He held her both hands and lifted half of her mask showcasing her pink lips and kissed her forcefully . The girl kept squirming and struggling in his grip but it was all useless. She kicked him where the sun doesn't shine and landed a kick with her long, sharp heels breaking his nose. This girl...

His nose was healed in no time and he moved his neck sideways to get a little serious. Will he kill her now like the other girls? He ran towards the girl and pinned her on the ground whispering something in her ear which I couldn't hear. When he was done with her, he removed her band sending her flying out of the ring. Then he walked towards Irene and removed her band as well.

******

Recap

Irene - Ivan's sister

Martin - Butler of Reese family

Claire - William's sister (now dead)

Issac - Ivan's brother (now dead) who was suppose to marry Claire.

Vincent - Claude's cousin brother

Ria - Scott Draken's cousin sister, member of council, winner of dart game against Serena

If still doubt, you can find the family flowchart in starting of 'Symbols' chapter

Chapter 26 - White Cult

William's POV

Rowan then made his way to another girl. No other vampire dared to go near him.

On the other hand, I could see the brunette in white cloak still safeguarded by her white cult. Surprisingly, none of them had a single drop of blood on their white cloaks. They didn't attack anyone just stood inert at a corner. Everyone else was too busy in their own fight to notice these women.

The man in jet black hair was carelessly walking around the ring. Many vampires ganged up on him but within the blink of an eye, their bands fell on the mud and their bodies vanished from the ring.

Whoever he was, he didn't look so intimidating but he was undoubtedly terrifically strong. I am sure of that...

"Who is that guy? He's not laying a finger and already managed to take down so many vampires?" Claude sounded astonsihed. He stopped sipping his wine and intertwined his palms deliberately watching his every movement.

"I'm wondering the same. I can't even sense his mana. Seems the boy has exceptional skills to mask it" I replied straight face.

"He's a man..." Anna chirped from behind already bewitched by the man's beauty. So were the other girls. I chose not to reply and let them continue ogling the muscled boy.

I noticed an angry mana next to me unmasking by the second.

It was Ivan.

He was on the verge of losing his restrain. His muscles clenched under his shirt. Already, he was angry because of Irene's condition who still laid unconscious. Now what...

I saw the creature that caught his anger. It was a little figure in covered in red.

Ria...

Ria was beating the pulp out of Leila and another girl. Both the girls laid still on the ground and she kept hitting them mercilessly. Both of them were very young, practically kids, may be a few years elder than Charles. I was glad he was not chosen. The girls were probably the youngest of the chosen lot. She held the blonde by her hair, " Well, now that I see you, you don't interest me anymore". She yanked her band and moved towards Leila.

Leila had a big hole in her abdomen and was healing very slowly due to the vast amount of blood she already lost. Her breathing was very shallow and she was on the verge of dying. She held Leila by her hair and made her already limp body stand on her knees. I felt anger rising in me as well but nothing there was I could do. Ria had a sinister smile on her face.

Every year she only targets females and kill them ruthlessly in a very brutal manner. If anyone who was worse than Rowan, it was her. She elongated her sharp nails and cut Leila's long blue hair. Sniffing her now cut hairs, a vicious smile crept on her face. " You look more pretty like this". I looked at Ivan who seemed furious, so did his kindred. Her next actions sent a shudder to my spine.

She shoved the cut hairs in Leila's mouth.

It was her...Not Rowan...

She murdered those young girls from before who had their hairs in their mouth.

This girl is crazy....

She was about to rip her heart when she was abruptly slammed on the ground. The whole court was silent including the competitors who were now looking at the white-cloaked.

"Mary, you are not supposed to kill her", the white cloaked turned her head towards the another woman of her cult, who had an authority laced in her tone. Undoubtedly, she was their leader. The other white-cloaks didn't leave the brunette's side and still stood like iron shields next to her, now in a triangular formation. Mary nodded at her leader and walked towards Leila. By this time, Ivan was slightly relieved but still worried for his cousin. All his kindred stood near the railing carefully watching the three girls. Mary went near Leila, tapped on her neck and legs, and removed her band. The next second Leila was in Ivan's arms. Ada rushed towards her and gave her some potion getting her somewhat stable.

Now, it was a showdown between Ria and Mary. I highly doubted Mary to win it, after all Ria had won a lot of tournaments previously. She was the most powerful fighter as good as Levi. Probably, better than him and she was getting powerful at a faster pace. I could see her lean muscular body that she built in all these years. Compared to her, Mary was nothing but bones. The outcome of this match was clear...

Mary will die...

"Every time, every tournament, I see you killing innocent girls brutally, in a sinister way. You have no idea how much I despise you. I couldn't participate all these years, but this time, I'll make sure you learn your lesson", Mary announced in a furious voice.

Hearing this, Ria just laughed and continued laughing like a lunatic, "You would beat me? You? Wearing that thing?" and she continued rolling on her stomach with all the mud sticking to the thick blood on her clothes. Mary kept looking at her with a straight cold face. Ria swiftly moved towards her with her nails out and marked it towards her chest. Mary didn't flinch. She kept standing there without dodging. My eyes landed on her chest. She was unhurt. She caught Ria's wrist and twisted it. The latter let out a loud shriek. I saw the ions. By this time, all the ions were standing in their private space, watching the fight. Ivan let out a smirk. Claude and the others seemed surprised and satisfied.

I saw Ria's other arm in her clutches as well. So fast...When did she do that? And then...

She slapped Ria...

Smack...

Smack...

Smack...

She continued slapping and slapping her. Smack after Smack...

Ria struggled to get out of her grasp but it was all futile. This was very very insulting for the council - the ions. Those bastards look like red tomatoes. Anger and Frustration was clearly visible on their pathetic faces. I saw Claude who was very pleased with whatever was happening. Ria's face was already covered in other's blood so I couldn't make out if she was bleeding or not. But I was sure she was. The whole arena was silent and only the loud smacks on her cheeks could be heard. Mary kept smacking her like a rag-doll. Eventually, she stopped struggling and collapsed on the ground.

Mary elongated her sharp nails. I knew she wouldn't kill Ria because her leader had said so. "What are you doing? No...No..." Ria screamed in horror.

I didn't feel an ounce of pity for her. She deserved this. Everyone though she might do the same to her, cutting her hairs like she did to those young girls but instead she did something else, which stunned everyone. Mary carved a word on her forehead,

'SHAME'

By this time, all the ions were fuming in anger. Their mana's were off the charts. This was the ultimate humiliation to the council. All the spectators had mixed expressions. Some were shocked, some were curious about the white-cloaks, many of them very happy with the outcome. The jet black haired man sat and watched the women doing the deed. Even Rowan didn't interfere but had an amused look on his face. Even those two were enjoying this...

As soon as she was done carving, she removed Ria's band and quietly moved towards her cult completing the previous formation around the brunette.

"That was hilarious" Claude chuckled earning a glare from Scarlett.

"Indeed" I whispered back. Who would have thought this would be so interesting...

As soon as she was done, the rest of them continued with their fights filling the arena once again with screams and wails. Very few vampires were left now. I watched Rowan as he dangerously moved towards Rose and my heart was anxiously pounding against my ribs.

"Now now...what do we have here?", he slowly moved towards her.

This is not good. Jared stood next to her but he was no match for Rowan. I stood up tensed looking for Levi, he had his hands full with Nicolas. What a timing!!

This can't be happening...

Oh no...Get away from him somehow...

Anyhow...

Just go...

I felt my kindred all tensed, so was I, on seeing him advancing towards them.

" Where were you hiding, love?" Rowan slid his tongue over his lips leering at Rose, closing the distance between them. Rose was practically quivering in fear as Jared protectively tucked her behind him.

"Get away from her" Jared spotted on him.

"Aren't you the brat from William's house?", he gave him a disgusted look. Cecily stood in front of them out of nowhere. Thankfully...she was strong. She could hold him for sometime may be...

"Leave her alone Rowan" she stated furiously.

"I must say William have a good eye selecting his women", he smirked at me and I just returned an angry glare. The next moment, Rowan flew towards Rose and held her hand but Jared managed to get in between.

"NO" I screamed...

My kindred we all screamed and stood up...

Rowan took no time to bury his fist in Jared's chest knocking him unconscious. While his hand was still in his chest, he gazed towards the audience, towards me and shouted...

"Should I kill him William?", he smirked at me. His expression was devious, completely evil. All I could do sitting here was stare daggers at him.

The next moment Cecily landed a chop at Rowan's neck making him loose his balance and he became slightly dizzy. He slowly removed his hand from his chest, luckily without his heart, and stepped away from Cecily.

"Cassandra, Eva, be ready with your potions", I said and they nodded getting those from their bags.

"You bitch, what did you do", he sat on his knees swearing profanities at Cecily, while she continued striking him. I was completely astonished. What was that move? It seemed she hit an important pressure point of his and her movements were not like others. They were more like a martial artist. Rowan got up and recovered in no time and sparred with her. He was not completely serious, he was just playing with her. In between his moves, he was taking his sweet time caressing her and touching her. But it was getting difficult for him with her weird ninja moves.

On the other side, Rose was weeping near Jared's unconscious body. She shaked him but he didn't woke up. I could sense his mana depleting and leaving his body at a faster rate. He was dying. Suddenly, I saw Nicolas coming towards them. Where's Levi??? I thought to myself and saw him circled by Valac's goons. This is so bad. I felt so pathetic and useless myself, seeing them like this and couldn't do anything. He lifted Rose by her hair and knocked her out in a single blow. I thought this was for the better if he just removes her band but he had no intention of letting them go so easily. He started kicking her brutally.

That Son of a b*tch...

As soon as Levi saw this, he became furious. Rage seeped out of his mana. He knocked out all the men removing their bands and move towards Levi in his bloody form. There was a big hollow in his chest and blood was gushing out, but he was only bothered by what was happening with Rose. Her whimpers were only thing he was hearing now.

His eyes grew dark, pitch black and all he craved was his blood.

Nicolas's blood...

He was a strong fighter when it comes to raw muscle power, probably stronger than me. He can easily defeat Nicolas. But he was in no shape even to kill an average vampire. By this time, Rose was also unconscious next to Jared.

"So this is the slut for whom you left my daughter and went with Claudius", Nicolas spoke pointing towards Rose. Wait...What is he saying...What does it mean...I gazed at Claude who seemed very tense and I felt him stealing his eyes from me. And I knew what they are talking about.

Levi loves Rose.

How can I be blind all these years. They were always together. He always use to be around her even knowing she loved Jared. I thought they were best friends. He was the one who brought her to the palace in the first place. Later she fell in love with Jared. I heard a few rumours about them. Some being Rose is cheating Jared, some being they all have a nasty threesome, some even being Levi has romantic feelings towards Jared...Now it was all clear...He loved Rose not Jared...

All vampires having sensitive hearing could hear this little confession of our lover boy...I could hear my kindred already gossiping forgetting the gravity of the situation.

"You made a big mistake touching Rose. You'll pay with your life" Levi fumed in anger and walked towards him. Blood was oozing out of his chest and his face was getting pale by every passing moment. Nicolas landed a kick on his abdomen but he dodged it. Levi swiftly moved his palm inside Nicolas's chest ripping his heart out.

Nicolas was dead...Yess...

By this moment, Levi's lungs were giving up on him. He took more damage than Jared. He sat near Rose took her in his arms.

What is he doing

He placed a kiss on her lips fainting over her. By this time, my kindred were screaming in awe seeing the public display of his affection. I chose to delete the scene from my memory. This is still not good. They are alive but still in danger. Their bands are still intact. I was losing my mind. I saw Cecily, she was struggling but still keeping up with Rowan. She didn't had any fatal injuries but she was completely exhausted. At this rate, she wouldn't last more than minutes...

I saw a movement near the white-cloaked women. The brunette whispered something and I could see her eyes welled up with tears. After that, Mary and the leader stayed guarding the brunette whereas the other two left her. The shorter girl went towards my three kindred who laid lifeless on the ground. She pinpointed her finger and pressed at Levi's chest and neck and his feet. She did the same with Jared. She didn't do anything to Rose. And then, she removed all their bands sending them to us.

I turned around to found them unconscious. Claude stood near Levi and was very tensed seeing him in this condition.

"Cassandra please, save him" he pleaded her.

"Those women have pressed their vital points slowing down the blood flow. It'll give us more time to save them" she replied and poured her potion in both their mouths. Eva handled Rose. She didn't had any fatal injuries and I was glad all three of them came back alive. Thanks to the white-cloaked women. Now only Cecily is left...

The taller white-cloaked woman went towards Cecily and Rowan. She landed a kick on Rowan's face and held Cecily's arm which was ready to pound into Rowan, "You cannot continue anymore", she said to Cecily and removed her band swiftly and returned to her formation. Cecily was sent flying back to us.

"What just happened? Who was she?" was all she said, "she saved me, who are these women" Cecily exclaimed in shock.

By this time, the rest of the vampires were defeated by the jet black-haired person. Only he, the five white cult women and Rowan was left. Now, this was very confusing...Who would win...All these people have prove their worth...And even I cannot say who would win...

Only the strong would survive...

Chapter 27 - Winner

Serena's POV

Terror overtook my senses when Rowan stepped closer to us.

My body was practically shaking and I held Resmelda's hand in fear.

My heart was threatening me to jump out of my chest.

My soul already left my body seeing him advancing towards us.

On the other hand, it was Lucas. I was shocked to see him here. He too was a vampire, a strong one. Luckily, I had my mask and cloak on. Rowan didn't recognize me. Nobody did...

"Never knew I would see you in this ring, Hilda?" Rowan spoke facing towards us. He stood still in his spot tunneling his fingers through his hairs.

He knows them...

"Not that you have to know. Why did you enter?" Resmelda questioned him back while his face had a smirk.

"Let's say a little birdy whispered in my ear, I would meet someone interesting here. Never imagined, I would meet you all ladies here. But who is the pretty addition to your quart, and why does she seem so weak" he snickered looking at me. I flinched and directed my eyes on my shoes.

Oh no...Don't come close...

Stay away...Stay away...

Seeing him off guard, Lucas rushed towards Rowan and caught his arm in an attempt to yank his band. But Rowan freed himself smoothly and moved away, "Not so fast..." he smirked. Lucas seemed very shocked.

"I don't want you frightening these women", Lucas said in stern face.

Rowan just laughed, "These women are not at all scared. You'll see what I mean when you take their punch". It seems Rowan knew their strength and was being very vigilant with the girls unlike with the others.

"Mary, Sussane take those two...Do not kill them" Hilda commanded the two girls. I had witnessed Rowan's strength first hand. Even William, Ivan and Claude together were no match for him. How will any of them would be able to take him down. I am very worried for them...

Mary went to Lucas whereas Sussane went to fight Rowan.

"Really Hilda, this kid? You think I'm so weak? I don't think anyone here in this arena is a good competition for me except you" he sounded annoyed at her.

"I know how strong you are Rowan. But its not only you, who have been training all these centuries", Hilda said.

"Is that so? We will see then" he smirked and stretched his neck and shoulders. For the first time, I saw him warming up. Sussane flew towards him gracefully and with a phenomenal speed she grazed his neck. Rowan settled down but managed to get up and moved away from her. It was a similar move that Cecily pulled off. He was collapsed on his knees and breathing hard.

"Not those crazy moves again" , he stood up and moved around at a supersonic speed around Sussane. I felt Resmelda tensing up next to me. Sussane was dodging his attacks like they were nothing. Both were equal. None of them landed any severe attack on the other. The scene was like two equally strong people are fighting not to hurt each other - which was not true in this case.

Both went for the kill...

The next moment Rowan vanished and pinned Sussane on the ground. He hovered over her, "You aren't training enough, kid ", he said smirking at her whereas Sussane was growling and struggling beneath him. He took off her band and defeated her...

Sussane was defeated...

On, the other hand it was the same. Mary was keeping up with Lucas perfectly. Her movements were very graceful. "You should give up. I don't like to hit women", Lucas stated earning a growl from all my girls even from Hilda.

The feminist side of me was a bit annoyed at his comment. A part of me wanted Mary to defeat Lucas.

I have been with them for more than two months now. And the one thing that was clear to me was they despise men to their core. Resmelda never said me why...All I knew they were feminists and had absolute hatred towards the opposite sex. They firmly supported the concept of misandry...

"Such audacity..." Resmelda blabbered in anger.

Mary took a large breath and her black eyes turned pitch-black. She was angry. Her movements were fast almost invisible. She was fast, freaking fast. Lucas increased his speed as well. He had no sweat keeping up with her. She slapped, kicked and punched him as he was trying hard to dodge her.

He was going to be defeated I'm sure. "I never doubted you were strong. You have proven that. Needed you catch you off-guard. But now its enough. See ya" saying this Lucas smirked and vanished. He tricked her. He didn't mean those comments and I was happy for that but that was a sly move.

Where the hell did he go?

Mary kept searching for him and in another moment she also vanished. What's this trick?

I saw there was a commotion among the spectators near pillar 24. I was shocked to see Mary sitting there in the audience, without her band, furiously hissing at the ring and trying to re-enter the ring. Sussane had to grasp her and calm her anger.

Mary was defeated...

I saw Resemelda who was shocked but Hilda had a calm face. It seemed like she already knew the outcome.

I saw Hilda approaching towards the Lucas. Now, I was being guarded only by Resmelda.

"Resmé sweety, Hilda seems busy and if you don't want me to come there and fight with you and your weak little friend, you better come here" Rowan announced eyeing me.

Resmelda seem furious and hesitant to leave me vulnerable. I was the reason, they entered this fight. "Stay here. Don't move. We won't let any harm come to you". I nodded and obeyed her commands whereas Resmelda walked towards Rowan.

Ivan's POV

The Resmelda girl made a slit in her dress till her waist to get some space. I could see those tan sexy legs even from here. She must be sexy in person. She was getting ready for the fight.

She moved at an immense speed and punched right into his face. He wasn't able to dodge. She landed another two kicks back to back in his abdomen. He was blown away and was writhing in pain.

"I must admit. You've gotten strong from the last time" Rowan mumbled as he got up and increased his mana. It was freaking powerful. Never have I ever seen him like this. Now that I compare him with the day he fought with us, that was nothing. This girl must be strong, stronger than us for him to get serious.

He kicked her back.

I had never seen Rowan hitting any girl. And he kicked her...

She was unfazed. She swirled around her toe and attacked him back. He caught her before she could land another powerful kick, "Sorry Resmé, as much as I want to defeat you, I won't today. I want to see your kitten and then we can continue our fight. I won't disband you", he whispered and pressed his finger too harshly on Resmelda's neck.

Cecily and Sussane's move. He learnt it...

In such a short time

She fainted on the ground. With a swift speed he moved towards the brunette white-cloak girl and caught her by her waist.

"Who are you, love? That compelled the 'No-Names' into this fight" Rowan whispered in her ear. She was cowering in fear and was about to collapse on the ground but he caught her and made her stand. All the eyes were on her.

He wanted to unmask her...

He wanted to see her face...So did I...

So did everyone in the arena...

The mysterious white women who entered only for this girl, willing to sacrifice their life for this girl and were filthy strong on equal terms with Rowan. I need to see. I need to know.

No-Names...

"Rowan, I'll kill you if you harm her" Hilda screamed at him leaving black wigged man and moving towards Rowan but was stopped by him. I just want her to snatch his wig and expose him. I don't understand why didn't anyone see through his get up yet. Not even that idiot Rowan. If only he was not blinded by the women...

The man had a fake cheap quality wig on his head. And I am pretty sure his eyes are also lens. He didn't try hard to hide his persona. But everyone is too distracted to check him out...Morons

"Trust me Hilda, I don't wish to die by your hands. And I'll not harm her. Just want to see your new friend", he smirked earning a scornful look from Hilda.

By this time, Rowan already held the string of the girl's mask in his hand, "Lets see your beautiful face" and he slowly removed it along with my cloak.

"Rowan NO...." Hilda screamed but the mask was ou...Serena?? What the hell??

"Lottery...I never in my wildest dreams expected you to be here...ki tty" Rowan said with widened eyes.

"Serena" I saw Claude and the others screaming.

"Serena, what the hell are you doing here" I heard the wigged man and Hilda gazed him back in shock. He knows her too...

"Lucas..." she whimpered. She knew him.

"Where were you Serena? I was going insane finding you from last two months" Lucas replied. Why is he saying what we are supposed to say. Thankfully, she's found but that bastard has her...I went down near the edge of the ring so were Claude and William.

"I...I.." words were not forming in her mouth knowing Rowan still had his hands all over her. By this time, it was a chaos in the whole arena.

"You bastard, get your filthy hands off her" Claude screamed from next to my side. His mana was dangerously rising by the second. This is not good...

"If you even touch a strand of her hair, you'll die. Leave her right now" Lucas spouted in anger as well.

What's with him

"What have you done, kitty? All the men and even these women are in love with you. It just makes me wanna fight them all off and have you for myself" he tightened his grip on her waist.

Claude was going totally crazy outside. The earth was shaking in tremors and slowly things were levitating in the air through his abilities. All the Valacs had their eyes on Claude and Serena. They were shocked knowing he has such a powerful mana and now even abilities.

"Cease the Fight" Vincent ordered and everyone stopped, "Felicia, remove the barrier".

The translucent barrier was slowly removed and within a second Claude, William and I entered the ring. I saw the white-cloaked defeated girls entering from the opposite.

"Liam capture the human girl and kill her" Vincent commanded Liam and Liam moved towards Rowan and Serena. Claude hissed at him in anger and directed all the floating objects at him. Liam moved his arms and all the objects vanished. He opened a dimensional portal sending all the things inside.

I stood with William forming a defensive positions before Liam could reach Serena.

Lucas released an electric shock towards Liam which he sent into another portal.

As he came close to Rowan, Rowan dodged with Serena along with him. The rest of us guarded them both.

"Felicia, chain everyone down there" Vincent roared in anger and the next moment all of us had silver chains on our arms. No way....

My arms were burning. It felt as if someone had poured molten lava on my wrists. Collapsing on ground, I saw William who has collapsed too along with Lucas, Rowan, Claude and all the white-cloaked women. Liam caught Serena who was the only one without any chains and took her. Hilda was the only one standing. She had her silver cuffs but it was like she was unaffected. She broke them easily like they were nothing.

No doubt she is the strongest. Who is she...

"I need the girl" she announced.

"This human had trespassed here and known our secret. She has to die" Vincent spatted. That man was nothing but evil. I saw Claude who was clenching his fists in anger. The chains were not just normal silver otherwise he could have easily broken them. She enchanted them.

"Leave her Vincent" Claude said attempting to break his cuffs.

"Kill her"

"Leave her Vincent" Lucas screamed in anger.

I turned my head around to find my mother coming down. "This human is very important for our ritual. She's a part of the prophecy to get our moonstones back. Leave my son at once" Great she spilled the beans...

"Diana please tell your son..." my mother pleaded her sister. Seeing her sister bowing in shame, she turned towards the councill. We are all doomed. Its over...

"I ask the elders to judge our situation. We need this human to get our stones back. And it would be very unfair if the current royal family doesn't want to share the power. Kindly provide us justice" she cried faking her tears. She's good at this, cunning and a great actress but I highly doubt it'll be useful.

But now that she had asked help from council, even Valacs cannot interfere.

I saw Kyle descending from his seat along with Maya and Alticus. All three of them wore black suit. I was surprised to see Kyle not in his usual red robe.

"The human had entered our sacred festival. The women in white cloaks have brought her here. The Gregors and Reese hid the human all along. All of them are at fault" Maya announced and we all were still wriggling in pain on the ground. "Our lord would decide their fate."

We are officially going to be doomed.

The ions are going to destroy us all within blink of an eye. I hope Kyle at least let Serena go free...

Kyle stepped back and "Welcome everyone, my son, Scott Draken, the new lord of the council ".

All eyes were about to bulge out of their sockets as he appeared in his red robe. Even the Valacs were shocked. When did this happen...

"I am proud to be the new lord of the council as of today" he stated "First, bring the human here Liam". Liam had to obey. Vincent had a scorn look on his face. He didn't like the existence of ions. Someone with more authority, and more power than him. Liam took Serena and stood near him. She was on the brisk of a mental breakdown moving from one of her tormentors to another.

" Now, Queen Evelyn. Do not worry. There would be absolute justice" he smiled at my mother and continued , "The human has committed a big mistake entering our sacred festival. But since she is essential to get the other Royals get their stones back, we would not kill her" Vincent hissed in anger, unhappy with the verdict.

"But the human being here and hiding her existence from the council was a mistake from the Gregors and the Reese, so their punishment is they cannot keep the human with them anymore. She will stay with the council and can only meet the two families only when there's some news on the moonstones or any ritual to be performed.

The one who bought the human in this festival against our laws are the white-cloaked women. You have committed treason for which you deserved deaths but since this human is so useful for Royals, I am reducing your punishment. You all need to give out your identity as a punishment. And do not lie. I can detect it" Scott finished smirking towards us.

Even he was the one among those, who knew Serena's truth, but blabbering that would only lead to all ur deaths. In a way, he is saving our ass. But keeping her with him at the same time, that f*cker.

"How can we guarantee her safety in the council" Hilda asked.

"I guarantee. I wouldn't bring any harm to her" he replied.

"I don't agree. I am neither with the Gregors nor with Reese and Valacs had already disowned me. So I would come and meet her everyday", Claude furiously screamed.

Scott's face had a devilish grin, "That makes you a rogue. And the council doesn't appreciate the rogues entering their home. So back off" he arrogantly stated.

"Claude" Serena shouted tears falling freely from her eyes.

"Serena..."

"I don't want to go with him Claude, Hilda" she sobbed moving here eyes over us. I felt so angry seeing her like that. But we are all helpless against the council.

"Dont worry Serena. I can tell he doesn't lie. He speaks truth. And by all respect, I think lord has not said anything about us entering the councill. We would meet you there", Hilda stated assuring Serena. What is she even thinking. I being a King, a Royal, never got an entry over there. Only ions and those who are called by council themselves are allowed to enter.

"I think you don't understand rogues. The councill is a place only ions can enter as they please and rest all can enter only if our lord has authorized which he had not" Maya interrupted.

The white cloaks saw each other and nodded. " We would now complete our punishments" Hilda said as she moved towards Resmelda, who was still unconscious. And brought her in her arms. The other two stood next to her.

"I am Hilda Drako, first descendant and daughter of Kaine Drako, ION BY BLOOD"

"This is Resmelda Drako, my younger sister, ION BY BLOOD "

"I am Mary Wyvern, sworn loyalty to house Drako, paternal cousins to Drako, daughter of Goza Wyvern, ION BY BLOOD"

"I am Sussane Wyvern, sworn loyalty to house Drako, daughter of Goza Wyvern, and ION BY BLOOD"

They finished introducing themselves. I dint heard a thing. My brain was only processing three words-

ION BY BLOOD

Thats not possible. The only ions known from last 2000 years are just Drakens. These women must be lying.

"Thats bullshit. Do you take us all for fools?" Kyle spouted in anger.

"The Drako and Wyverns were all killed by Tarragons in a revolt. And whatever was left of Tarragons was wiped by us. Do you have any evidence to support your claim" Alticus said in straight voice.

Hilda cut her knife and poured the blood on Felicia's hand. The latter chanted something and her next words left the whole council, whole arena shocked.

"She is an ion" Felicia declared.

"I still can't believe this. I am happy to know we have someone from our ancestors here. I want to know everything" Scott stated.

"Yes, my lord..." she replied.

I was still shocked. The Tarragons killed everyone from house Drako and Wyvern. The kings killed all the men and tortured their women to death. It was very cruel. The way those women were treated is etched into our history. I never knew there could be any survivors.

Scott gained everyone's attention and continued, "Lets move to the festival outcome now. Hilda and Resmelda have been disqualified due to their treason. Lucas tried to attack the royal family ignoring the King's power. So you too are disqualified. Hence,Rowan is the winner. Tell me Rowan what is your wish that I can fulfill?".

The outcome was either expected. But seeing Lucas and Hilda, I think Hilda would have won if not disqualified.

" I want Serena" Rowan declared. Both Lucas and Claude jumped to attack him but he dodged them both. I felt immense rage and fire was burning in my veins. How dare he...

Scott had an angry expression himself. Ofcourse that motherf*cker wants her for himself, "Didn't you hear? She stays with the council. Think of something else".

Rowan sighed and then smirked, "Ok. I need a little quantity of potion of Ahemkara."

What's that?

Scott had a horrified expression. So did most of council elders.

"Its no more with us. And that's the truth. Select something else" Scott spotted in anger.

"I wish to stay for one year with the council"

Chapter 28 – Mask

Unknown POV

"I beg you, please spare my babies" the farmer's wife pleaded while gripping my legs with her bloodied fingers making a futile attempt to prevent me from killing the newborns. She was young, she wasn't even that beautiful, else I might have taken my sweet time to kill her. She kinda reminded me of the old fat cook at the BloodStone's palace. Come to think of it, the cook was better in her youth.

I kicked her in the face and took one of the crying infants.

This was the ninety-ninth baby.

"Even the demons are on our side. We are lucky to have twins this time" keeping both the infants on the table, I took out the Book of Aradia and carefully turned its rusty old pages to the sacrificial spell.

"Now, will you step on it? I don't want to squander another hundred years for this BlackSun Festival. The eclipse will end in the next two minutes", my sister spat while savoring blood and absorbing youth from the farmer's eldest daughter.

I am tired of repeating myself again and again. It is not the blood that can get her the youth but the mana. She is enjoying her new so-called abilities to feast on blood. She can sometimes be cranky, especially when she's just getting impatient to get her hands on the power to come.

So was I.

I needed to hurry. These are the last two of the babies needed to complete our ritual.

I swiftly pulled the dagger from my coat. Their mother's wail continued louder and louder as I went towards them. But instead of the babies, I shoved it into their mother's chest. She shouldn't witness her children's brutal death. Her screams were annoying.

"Softy" she murmured under her breath while draining the young girl and I did the deed with her children as well.

The hundredth one is done.

"Take care of the corpses", she ordered and the servants came rushing and we got down from the altar and went into our main keep down the hallway.

"Keep your bloodied hands off my clothes. You'll ruin them" I screamed at her as she sat next to me wiping her hands on her gown.

"My bad", she used a spell and got herself clean and all dolled up asking the maid to get a mirror. Once she was done checking her appearance which was slightly younger than before, a smile of satisfaction glowed on her face.

Eternal Youth

Even after so many centuries, she has the same doctrine as those ancient witches. Beauty and youth was their only aim.

Stupid hags.

The other witches were waiting for us. Finally, our long wait is over and we can put our main plan to action. The damn brandy I was sipping did not affect me due to the adrenaline coursing through my veins.

"My lord, my lady, the festival has come to an end. The castles are blown up", a servant spoke gaping in fear looking at us.

"The mole has entered the council", my sister laughed with an evil glint on her face.

Serena's POV

The eclipse came up. The entire arena was cloaked in darkness. A beam of light emerged from the moonstone and dispersed into numerous beams going through all the vampires. It was just seconds, and more than half the vampires left the arena as soon as it was done. Suddenly, my head started feeling heavy and my vision got blurry. All I could see were distorted images and figures. I held Scott's hand for support. It must be the heatstroke.

As soon as the arena was cleared, only the royal families, council, and Rowan were left along with the dead bodies. There was also Lucas but I wasn't sure whether he belonged to any of the royals or council. There was an unnerving silence owing to the turn of events.

A minute before the eclipse they received unfortunate news of all royal castles being burnt to crisp.

"This is the work of the Bloodstones. Matilda and John are behind this", William smashed a boulder in a fit of rage. The injuries on his body were no longer there. He was completely healed so was Claude and everyone else.

"It could be the wolves as well", Rowan responded with a smirk on his face.

"Nobody asked your opinion" Claude busted in anger to which Rowan just smirked.

"Due to these unforeseen circumstances, we abide by the rules. The royals would stay with the council until their new castles are built again", Scott's father announced to which everyone nodded in agreement. Scott moved forward and was irked by this dramatic turn of events. He appeared calm on the outside but the grip of his fingers on my wrist was saying otherwise. I flinched in pain. Sensing that, he released his grip and composed himself.

Rowan moved towards me, "Your fan club is very persistent in stalking you like shadows" he smirked and took a seat on the plush velvet couch stretching his legs while enjoying the show. I didn't dare to comment back neither did I intended to. "Don't worry kitten, if this turned into a fight, I'll protect you. I won't take part in the gore" he whispered in my ear.

Ya, right. You had already done your part in the arena.

" We need to increase the security for the remaining moonstone", Vincent expressed his concern. It was indeed crucial for it could wipe the existence of the entire vampire race. The current one belonged to Valacs. Seeing William and Ivan's family are still alive suggests the other two stones are still intact.

"Ok. It is settled then", I heard someone say before I fainted into oblivion.

****

I woke up in a completely different room. It had beautiful lilac walls with huge french windows. A bunch of white lilies laid in a cute little vase near the table. It was very soothing. A very familiar rancid smell with a hint of coffee struck my nose. I changed my side to see what it was only to be startled by the demon sitting on the chair gazing right at me.

"I didn't realize the moonstone would affect you as well. You were unconscious for two days. Are you feeling better now?", Scott said as he kept ogling at me. Impulsively, I took the sheets and covered my chest, and moved away from him. I just hate him more than Rowan. I despise him for what he tried to do last time.

"Why are you here?" I kept a straight face and asked him to keep my fear in control. I don't want to show him my inner demons.

"I'll take that as a yes", he kept the coffee mug on the table, "it's mixed with some medicinal herbs. I had it made especially from Cassandra. And it is safe to drink", he chuckled while moving the curtains aside. The rays coming from the sun pricked my eyes but it was warm here, much warmer than at Williams' palace.

Come to think of it..., "Where am I? Where is everyone?", I started panicking at the thought of me being here alone with this disgusting person.

He smirked, "Calm down. You are at my palace. Your friends are also here in the neighboring towers". I let a sigh of relief. However, he was just roaming leisurely around the balcony. Why is he not leaving? "How do you know Zephyr?", he suddenly asked out of the blue.

Who is that? What is he talking about? "Who?", I asked.

He let out a long breathe while still gazing outside the window, "Oh yes, you fainted right in my arms that time so you wouldn't know. Apparently, the one who disguised himself or rather who you know as Lucas is Zephyr Valac".

No way. The prince in hiding

And I fainted in Scott's arms.

His words were buzzing in my head like a cluster of obnoxious bees. I stuttered while answering him back. I felt enraged and embarrassed, " he met me at the party", I answered quietly.

Suddenly, he turned back, "I see, I am glad to see you are here well and safe. A maid would come with a few clothes for you. The breakfast would be held in the garden". It felt like he is talking to me but still, he is thinking something in the back of his mind.

"I'll see you", and he left the room.

I took a bath and got ready in the blue knee-length flare dress. It was chiffon and pretty comfortable. As I went downstairs towards the garden, I noticed how this castle was different from William's. It had that ancient rusty touch to it. But was still unique in its way. The garden spread across a huge green lawn with two big tables. I saw everyone was there including Claude. Cecily, Levi, and Rose were there as well. And they seem healthy. Everyone was sipping some wine, although a few of them had some bread and pudding. I wonder if vampires could eat normal food.

As soon as Claude saw me, he came running towards me and embraced me. I felt the heat rising through my cheeks due to this embarrassment. I was happy, no, more than happy to finally see him. Be with him. I got drown in the ocean of his eyes. For a moment, I forgot if there was anyone around us. Rose cleared her throat and we came back to reality.

"You look more gorgeous when you blush", he said pulling a strand of my hair behind my ear and he made his way towards the table and I followed and took a seat next to Rose.

"You both feel good now?" I asked Rose and Levi who were busy gulping their drinks.

"Yes, we were badly injured but thanks to the BlackSun, we recovered very fast", she replied while Levi refilled his glass. Seeing him, bought a smile to my face. He is so completely in love with her. Many of William's people were missing. And even some from Ivan's. "Where are Jared, Cecily, and others?"

Rose was sipping yet another glass. By this time it was around her fourth. She must be very hungry or thirsty. "They've been assigned to guard the moonstone with the others from Reese and Valacs".

And there goes the fifth one.

"Oh.."

******

I was allowed to roam freely in the main building. Much to my disappointment Claude and the others were not allowed. Hilda and the girls also left this morning since they were not used to such a lifestyle. Though Resmelda promised she would visit me in few days. I wished them to stay but apparently, Hilda suggested they had some important work to do and had to leave. In all the months, I've been with them, all that they did was meditate or train. It has to be something important.

I didn't realize when I came to the end of the stairs. There was a big hallway with paintings on either side of it. There were many from the

Renaissance era. Most of them had their family members. There was also one of the entire Draken Family including a small red-haired girl next to Scott's father. Scott was nowhere to be seen.

The next few were portraits from each royal family even Blood-Stones. And after seeing this, I realized what William always said was true. The King was indeed a madman. At least he looked like one.

The next one was a portrait of a bird, a beautiful bluebird. It had a long tail with fluffy plumage. I'm sure I saw one from these species back at William's. Like all the other paintings, even this one was named in some strange ancient script.

"zîv hêv. Is its name", a husky voice whispered in my ear. And the owner of this voice was more obnoxious and awful.

"You can read this?", I asked him. He was still in that careless attitude while he moved towards the painting and carefully watched it as if he's analyzing it.

" Seems you don't fear me anymore " he chuckled and I realized I should not test the waters and maintain a distance. My heart started pounding faster and it was now difficult to stop panicking. "Or maybe not", he added. I guess he heard it.

"So what does it mean?", I tried changing the course of our discussion.

"It says silver moon. The bird is a symbol of the same from the moon deity as they say. Although it usually is a white or a silver bird not blue", Rowan answered while still looking at the portrait. He seemed deep in thought.

"The artist might wanna be creative", I blurted in response and mentally slammed myself why did I cut him.

"He can but for this picture, I'm not so sure. Sometimes what we see, is not always true kitten. Like you see this picture", he pointed towards a portrait of a girl's back who had a mask in her hand, numerous masks laid down on the floor causing a trail of masks and she was walking into darkness.

"What do you think of this?" he took a step back giving me space to check the portrait carefully.

"I think it means you wear a mask for so long and you forget who you were beneath it", I answered to which he just laughed like a maniac.

" You're so naive. That's what I like about you. You see what I think is it means, people normally expose only a small part of themselves, and generally just the part they wish to show. People seldom change. Only their masks do. It is only our perception of them and the perception they have of themselves that change. Let me throw in one more piece of advice for you kitty" he paced towards me and whispered in my ear, "Even when changing masks, the girl is still showing her back taking utmost precaution to hide her true face, her true intentions. The palace is filled with such people now. A trap awaits in every corner. Be careful on whom you trust".

" What are you doing here, And how did Scott allowed you to roam free?" Cecily popped out of nowhere and Rowan vanished in a blink.

"It's just in the halls. Has everyone else come here as well?" I asked in desperation seeing Cecily here.

"Nope"

****

Chapter 29 - Attack

The next few days I only got to see Claude at the breakfast and sometimes for dinner. We would spend the time sitting next to each other and talking. I was happy. Life felt content and fulfilling. I frequently saw Cecily in the council. Apparently, her husband was one of the main members of the council. He was killed by Bloodstones in the skirmish. She was still a part of the council but loved to stay with William since she felt his place like home.

As I was leaving back to the main hall after dinner, Irene stopped me along with her butler Martin.

"What do you want?", I asked her.

"Are you done whoring around? You better stay away from Claudius. He is mine. Now that he had got his powers, he will be the king and

I would be his queen. Just get that straight in your head", before I could reply to her she pushed me hard and I fell down rolling and scraping my knees. She came towards me again and held me by my neck.

"Claude does not love you. He loves me. Just stop creating a scene and let go of me ", I managed to choke out those words in a faint voice. Her grip was tightening on my throat and my vision was getting blurry.

"Consider this my last warning. If you wish to live, stay away from Claudius. Because this time I will not have you pushed from a cliff but drink you dry", she whispered and left along with Martin.

"Yo...You tried to kill...", I was unable to finish my words, "And I will not hesitate to do it again."

I stood there completely frozen. I didn't know what to do.

******

I felt a cold breeze on my face and tip of my toes. As warm as if felt here during the day, it was equally colder in the night. The blanket didn't feel warm at all. It was getting chilly by every second. Suddenly, I felt hot air blowing near my toes. That was strange. The warm air slowly moved up and up travelling through my ankles and knees. It was as if someone is kissing me.I felt a light weight as if someone is hovering over me. He kissed me on my cheek and then again near my neck. It felt as if someone if suckling me. I tried to open my eyes and scream but I was unable to do so. Was it really someone or am I having a nightmare.

My heart started to pound very fast. My arms felt very weak. It was like a state of paralysis. I tried thrashing my legs but I wasn't able to move an inch. Whatever it was, had his hands all over me , exploring more. I couldn't take it anymore. I have to get up from this nightmare.

Gathering my full strength, I finally managed to wake up. My heart was beating like crazy threatening to jump out of my rib cage. Thanks to the dim lights, there was not complete darkness. There was no-body in the room. I felt a sigh of relief and switched the lights on. I need a glass of water. When I turned towards the table, I froze in shock and screamed as loud as I could.

A couple of moments later few guards along with Rowan and Zephyr came. There were some people from council as well along with Scott and his sister.

"What happen Serena?", I couldn't speak a word. I was completely horrified by the scene in front of me.

It was not my nightmare. Someone was indeed in my room. Whoever it was, left a message as well written with blood on the wall.

I will be back again, Love

" Who was it? Did you see anyone?", Zephyr asked me shaking my form trying to bring me out of my shocked stance. I simply nodded a No.

"I don't smell a mana nor any scent. I wonder who is capable of doing that? " Rowan stiffened while mumbling the same.

" I don't think it is some outsider. It is someone among...", his voice was cut by some skirmish going in neighboring castle.

A guard came running and bowed to Scott, "Master, Lady Irene was found dead in the woods".

****

Its been a week past Irene's death. Nobody knew who killed her. I didn't see her body but Rose was saying she was attacked by a wolf. The claws were poisonous and dug deep into her heart. All the breakfasts were served in everyone's room. I didn't even get to see Claude from that day. Cecily was the first to find her body. Ivan's mother blamed her for Irene's death. What grudge would she be holding against her. I don't think it is Cecily. Things are pretty awkward now among everyone.

I was sitting in the garden when Rose and Levi came towards me.

"Hi" she waived.

"Hey".

"Red wine?", she offered me a glass. I was sceptical about taking it whether it was blood wine or red wine. Also, I was not into liqour but tonight I felt like having some.

I hesitantly took over the glass, " Where are you headed to?"

"Its Jared's shift to guard the stone today. So we just thought to stop by", she replied awkwardly. I also wanted to go somewhere instead of wandering in this limited space but I was not allowed. Both of them left. And I just stayed there sitting in the dark empty garden.

A couple of minutes later, I felt a presence. It was as if I'm being watched.

****

Please vote if you like

Chapter 30 – Him

The last few days were very hectic. Security was very tight since Irene's death. A cross mark in molten silver was branded on the ground next to her bloody corpse. I didn't see with my own eyes but from what I heard, it was a gruesome view. The culprit intentionally did this to send some kind of hidden message or a threat. I wonder how did a wolf enter the territory and left unnoticed.

Ivan's mother lost her sanity following the demise of her daughter. I cannot imagine the agony she must've felt losing yet another child to death. Though she was grieving, her raging desire for revenge kept her sanity in check but still, everyone turned a blind eye to the concoction of black magic she was brewing with Ada to get her hands on the murderer. Cassandra and all the witches tried the same when Irene was killed but their attempts were in vain.

Claude also did not come to see me since then. Apparently, his new-found levitation ability had brought 'newfound arrogance' with it. Nowadays, he doesn't talk to me normally. Whenever I see him, he just ignores me and plots with William on how to get back control on Valacs since he is the rightful heir now. Zeref on the other end is also no different. With both of them back, there is a severe imbalance in the power dynamics for the throne.

Rose and Jared are also busy in their own lives, I get bored out of my mind sitting here alone in misery. The only people who pay me a regular visit are Rowan and him.

Sleep was also not easy. Every day is torture. He comes here every night, suckles my neck, and leaves me confused. When he is here, I cannot open my eyes and cannot fight back. My body ultimately surrenders to sleep paralysis, to him.

Guards have been assigned outside my room, but they never see anyone entering the room. They claim I've gone insane and now, even I'm starting to doubt my sanity. I am beginning to lose my mind. It is playing tricks on me.

These hallucinations are getting unbearable every passing day.

Nothing feels real.

I don't know who it is.

I was sleeping, but it felt like I'm not. All power and life were being sucked out of my body. I didn't know what was happening.

The familiar touch, the familiar aura, is back again.

He is back tonight as well. His cold fingers slithered from the nape of my neck to the valley of my chest. His lips skimmed my neck leaving a trail of wet kisses tracing passionately from my ear to my clavicle.

The touch felt inappropriate as I felt a sharp pain near my neck. I wanted to scream but all that left my mouth was just air. I don't know what it is, whether some vampire drinking my blood and killing me, or is it just a dream.

His hard chest struck my soft ones, grinding against my bosoms, caging me in the prison of his solid arms. The masculine cologne invaded my senses as he violated my lips. The metallic taste of blood lingered on my tongue as he tasted it again hungrily.

I need to stop him.

I need to stop myself.

I attempted to lift my hands but I lacked the will to break through this nightmare.

After what felt like forever, I woke up startled, panting like a crazy person. Moonlight radiated the dim room easing me to find my way towards the door. I threw my legs across the bed and searched the entire room, but there was no one. I open the large door and saw the same two guards outside. Their dull, lifeless eyes had an annoyed expression. Of course, they must be thinking, I am a madwoman.

"Did you see anyone coming in?"

They shook their heads without sparing a glance to me.

"Are you sure?"

Their reaction was dark, furious and I knew why. A mere human questioning their super skills and abilities infuriated them and now was clearly visible in their eyes which were black now like deep dark black.

They thought I am nuts.

But the stinging sensation in my neck was very real.

The touch was real.

I am sure somebody comes here every day.

Everyone urged me to take a rest. They think it's simply nightmares. Everyone was convinced about it. Hell, even Claude doesn't believe me. They believe if I was in danger, William and Ivan must have sensed, who didn't feel a thing. But I know I am not hallucinating. Someone do come here every day.

I went back within the safety of my room and slammed the door. After ensuring windows are closed, I lay on my bed and drift to sleep only hoping he doesn't return.

****

As soon as I stepped out of my room, the next morning, I saw Cecily lurking in the hallway restlessly pacing. As soon as she saw me exiting my room, she marched forward, her face straight and cold.

"What?"

She stood in front of me, her eyes pierced mine as if scavenging for some sort of answer or explanation. She's been acting strange lately especially after Irene's death. I noticed her around everyone especially me. I just hope she's not the murderer like everyone's accusing her.

Ok, something's really wrong with her.

Without feeling the need to answer me, she kept staring at me instead. Her eyes pressed on my neck for a second lingering near my chest and further down. Once she was done ogling, she moved at supersonic speed and vanished.

That was weird.

I walked across the long hall as I heard people shouting and arguing. I hurried downstairs skipping steps as fast as I could. The chairs laid overturned, some missing legs around the huge table which was now split in two. Claude raised the splinters of furniture up in the air ready to attack whereas Scott had a scowl on his face.

"There she is. Grab her and end this once and for all", Vincent ordered his guards while flashing his fangs at me. Unable to understand the situation, I instinctively stepped back clutching my skirt tightly.

Before his guards could take any action, William and Ivan decapacitated their heads.

"Do not dare, Vincent", Zephyr growled at him.

"I'll fucking kill you", Claude threw a few objects in the air aiming towards his cousin.

Everyone was flashing their fangs at each other ready to go all out. Hilda and the girls were also present securing their place next to ions. Over the last few days, they've been frequently visiting the council. They were very well admired by Scott and his family.

"If we don't hand this bitch over, it would be the end for us all, our whole damn race", Vincent shouted back furiously breaking the table into pieces.

Claude and Zephyr stood like a shield in front of me along with the witches. Scott stepped forward and declared, "What makes you think Matilda will not destroy the stones even after getting her hands on this girl. We need to plan this properly."

I was confused as to what happened in the middle of the night. By now, I was certain he meant me. Matilda has finally made her moves it seems. I waited and listened keenly to their arguments and opinions. There were too many egos clashing in this room making it difficult for everyone to come to a solid conclusion. Following the arguments, I deduced the cause of this sudden panic.

The Valac moonstone was gone.

Stolen in the dead of night by Matilda who demanded me in exchange for one of the stones. The existence of the vampire race was in question, no wonder Vincent was hell-bent on giving my head on a silver platter. All their kindred backed their leaders ready to attack. It's not good. I doubt now even Reese or Gregos would protect me. Also, even if they did, it will be pointless seeing their existence lies in her hands.

The argument went on and on, each party providing their opinions, ideas and even threats. So far none of it was agreed upon by everyone.

Claude wanted us to create my clone and use the same to hand it over to Matilda.

Zephyr was ready to go for an all-out war.

The council suggested handing me over.

William and Ivan, for a change, had nothing to say on the matter concerning me. All they wanted was to wreak havoc and avenge their family.

Hilda and the girls kept quiet in a corner unfazed by the loss of stones.

Vincent only wanted to get rid of me and wanted to get the stone back.

Rowan was missing since the morning, apparently, he fled.

Rose was crying while Levi comforted her. Jared was missing as well, either taken hostage or killed.

Unable to come to a conclusion, nothing came up. Everyone bickered amongst themselves opposing each other's idea. Finally, a voice broke off the squabbling garnering everyone's attention.

It was Hilda.

"I have a plan that would guarantee Serena's safety. Also, I would aid you fighting Matilda, however, I would require a lot of power in doing so hence, the retrieval of stone is something which must be taken care of by you all", she declared.

Everyone looks at each other's faces. They knew Hilda was fiercely strong and had even showcased her strength when she broke Valac's witch spell. They silently acknowledged her power and nodded their heads.
"If she's going to be fine, then fine by me", Claude stated.

"When do we leave?", William asked.

"By the nightfall"